Helping Hand for Ethan

Daniel Lance Wright

Credits

Cover Artist: Designs by MS G.
Editor: Ashley Tofte

Printed in the United States of America

Chapter One

"Yippee!" Unable to bridle enthusiasm, ten-year-old Ethan Lee whooped as the final bell rang. Summer vacation had just begun.

Students bottlenecked at the classroom door, laughing, shoving one another then spewing into the hallway like a shaken bottle of soda pop, cheering as they sped toward the front double doors.

He rode the wave, having no desire to stay in that classroom, in this school, for one more second. His feet carried him, but the streaming crowd kept him moving at a riotous pace to the waiting line of school buses in front of Plainfield, Texas Elementary School. Chewing his lip, he waited in line to get on his assigned bus. Finally, he got his turn and swung up into it by the handrail, flying over the first two steps, feet coming to rest on the third. Among the last on, he looked across the hyperactive jumble of grinning faces--not a sad sound in the crowd on this final day of school. He spotted his buddies, also classmates, Mikey Moore and Bubba Watkins. He couldn't distinguish their screams from the rest but his eyes locked onto four wild waving hands. Making a beeline, sliding sideways past smaller kids, he fell onto the saved seat, bumping Mikey, shoving him over. Mikey, in turn, pushed Bubba, squeezing him against the wall of the bus. "Hey," Bubba squawked, "Doggone it, ease up. That hurts."

Ethan squirmed then grinned at them both. "Sorry. Too excited. Can't slow down." He adjusted but still sat on the very edge, one leg in the aisle so the three of them would fit on the same seat.

Mikey's head bounced like a bobble-head doll. "Yeah, I know whatcha mean. What's the first thing you're gonna do when you get home, Ethan?"

"Head for the creek and go swimmin'; what else?"

Bubba's eyes grew large. "Ooh, cool." He then squinted and huffed. "Wait a doggone minute. That's not fair. We don't have a swimmin' hole."

Ethan noticed Bubba's older brother Aaron perked his ears when swimming was mentioned. He sat in the seat ahead of them.

Aaron turned. Before Ethan could react, the older boy thumped him on the forehead.

"Hey! Why'd ya pop me?"

"It's not fair. We wanna go swimmin' too."

He rubbed the reddening lump on his head and thought about it. "If it's okay with my parents, I'll have a party later this summer and invite all y'all over to go swimmin'. How's that?"

Aaron stabbed the air close to Ethan's nose. "Just don't forget you made the offer, twit." He flicked Ethan's nose then smirked before turning away to rejoin the ruckus by the older boys.

"I got it, but you gotta be nice. No more of that thumpin' stuff." The annoyed look disappeared as fast as it came on, right back to a grin.

The brakes on the old bus squealed as it came to a stop on the road in front of the Lee family farm. Ethan dashed through flailing arms and knees to the front of the bus. Everyone he passed shouted goodbyes, most with a slap or a pat on the back; some tried tripping him. He accepted it all as well wishes for a good summer. It'd be autumn before he saw most of them again.

The doors of the bus sprang open. He leaped out as the driver ground the over-worked old bus into gear, sounding like it needed a summer-long rest too. He watched it pull away belching black smoke. Mikey and Bubba crowded the open window. "See ya, Ethan. Don't forget the party." The bus and the noise faded in a distant cloud of brown Texas dust.

He stood for a moment in the utter silence of farm country, a wide open plain of seemingly endless farms and plowed fields speckled with farm houses. A twinge of regret seized him--but just a stitch, and only for a second, when he considered three months would zip by and he'd see them all soon enough.

Running from the road up the long driveway to the house, he could think of nothing other than getting down to the creek. He leaped up onto the back porch of his home and yanked open the back screen door shouting, "Momma, I'm home."

Without waiting for an answer, he shucked clothes as he ran to his bedroom, leaving a trail of shoes, socks, shirt and jeans. "I'm going swimmin' down at the creek. Okay?"

His mother, Faye, appeared at the bedroom door just as Ethan slipped into a faded and frayed pair of cutoff jeans. She had her straight brown hair pulled back and tied into a ponytail, wearing red Capri pants topped with a button-up white sleeveless blouse and a pair of flip-flops. She looked at him with a suspicious squint. "I suppose. But you be extra careful, ya hear? You're daddy isn't home and I'm too busy to keep an eye on you."

"Not a problem." With fingers moving in a fumbling rush, he zipped and buttoned his favorite cutoff jeans then scooted past her. "See ya in a little bit." He hoped she had nothing else to say. The lure of the creek and getting summer vacation underway swelled in him like a male toad in the hunt for a mate, responding as any ten-year-old would. The fast walk turned into a sprint once he dropped off the back porch. His feet barely touched the plowed ground between cotton rows as he ran down the hillside, mind and body in overdrive.

Without slowing, he burst through Chinaberry saplings at the creek bank and went airborne. "Yea!" He flew into the cool water, splashing high then swimming to the bottom. Noisy birds took flight in a startled rush from the many trees lining the creek.

Surfacing, he sprayed water from between puffed cheeks then swam across to his favorite hangout, the flat stone jutting out barely above the surface of the water and pulled himself up onto it. It was just below another stone protruding out even farther about six feet above where he sat. He called that one the "diving rock".

Sitting for only a short time, Ethan climbed to the higher surface, seven, or so, feet above the water. He took two quick steps toward the edge. On the final step, his heel came down on sharp rock chips, sending a burning pain through his foot.

His step stuttered.

Balance vanished as his feet shot out in front of his body.

He fell backward.

His head thudded against the edge as he went over.

He heard the splash but never felt the water closing over him.

He groaned, struggling to remember what'd happened then moaned and held his pounding head with both hands. "Oh, man..." He squeezed his eyes shut even tighter.

At that moment, all he remembered was the bus ride home. He lifted his head. It throbbed, feeling every beat of his heart in it. Eventually, he became aware of the sun shining through his eyelids and rolled onto his side, exploring the lump on the back of his head with walking fingertips.

Pain gave way to wonder. He finally remembered that he'd slipped and banged his head on the diving rock. He opened his eyes and saw water dripping from his body, pooling beneath him. He lay on the low jutting rock massaging the back of his head. *Wait a doggone minute.* He looked around but saw no one although water beneath the diving rock rippled, as if he'd just climbed from it. *I don't remember getting out of the water.* There was no other apparent reason for the water to be disturbed like that. It was a calm afternoon.

Trees up the creek reacted to a sudden wind gust. Branches waved his direction, on this otherwise serene afternoon. It seemed confined to the creek channel between the trees. A cool blast hit him--cooler than it should've been, even on a wet body. He shivered then watched trees downstream react as it blew on by.

Ethan didn't understand how he came to be safely upon the large flat rock above the water. He couldn't remember a thing after his head slammed the diving rock other than hitting the water's surface. Again he looked all around, wondering, but didn't feel like thinking too hard on it. *I'd better keep this to myself.* The only notion he latched onto without painful effort was that it was the first day of summer vacation and three solid months of good swimming weather ahead and didn't want to mess it up.

After the full impact of almost drowning sank in, the headache was now only part of the problem. He became nauseous and felt like vomiting. Swimming anymore today suddenly didn't seem like such a great idea.

Chapter Two

Late June

Ethan climbed dripping from Meandering Creek onto the low jutting rock plate and kept right on climbing to the higher overhanging rock shelf. On his way up, he stopped long enough to identify the sound of his father's approaching tractor beyond the chinaberry trees bordering the narrow waterway.

It reminded him to slow down and watch his footing. Remembering that close call in the spring, he picked a path over rough rocks that pressed the soles of his bare feet. He stood at the edge and looked down to the water's surface, about to dive when he heard the tractor come close and the engine die. He waited.

Pushing long, unkempt and sodden hair away from his eyes, he saw his father appear through the trees. "Hey, Dad, watch this." Taking two quick steps, he flew from the edge, clasping hands around his knees and tucking them into his chest. He'd accept nothing less than a record-setting cannonball. Water splashed high as he sank far below the surface. His feet touched the bottom on bended knees then shot back to the surface.

He swam to the low rock plate cut under by flowing water and climbed onto its sun-warmed surface. He pulled his sagging denim cut-offs up by a belt loop. "Am I gettin' good or what?"

Sliding down the short but steep embankment to the water's edge across the creek, his dad pulled off a green John Deere cap. Sandy blonde hair spilled from beneath the cap and hung at an angle above his eyebrows. He scratched his head, pretending to give it thought. "Well, son, I have three things to say about that." He dropped the cap, pulled a boot off then began dancing around, pulling the other off. "Number one, you really are getting good…number two, if you want to see your eleventh birthday, you need to be very careful when you're out here alone…and number three, I bet I can do better than that." He yanked his socks off and dropped his pants. Wearing only dark green paisley boxers, he dived in and swam across to meet Ethan on the rock.

"Yeah, right. I bet you can't beat it. But I sure wanna watch you try."

"Out of my way, boy, and watch an expert." He slid by Ethan and climbed to the top of the higher diving rock. Tiptoeing to the edge, Sid bowed to his audience of one.

Ethan pretended to have a microphone to his mouth. "And now, ladies and gentleman, Sid Lee will attempt to break Ethan Lee's world record in the cannonball."

With an ear-splitting yell of, "Geronimo!" Sid took off and leaped high, leaving the edge a touch too powerful, form far from perfect. He rolled backwards Abandoning tradition, he opted for the I-think-I'll-flail-my-arms-and-legs style, managing to keep from slapping the water with the flat of his back, employing a comical twisting motion.

Ethan laughed until he could laugh no more and then announced, "And the record for the best cannonball in Meandering Creek in the great Lone Star state of Texas remains with the boy on the rock." He bowed to his father and then to an imaginary audience.

Sputtering and gagging from water driven up his nose, Sid climbed up and sat next to Ethan. They shared a laugh.

After a time, Sid looked to the sun's position in the sky. "Your momma'll be mad if we don't get back up to the house for supper pretty soon."

"Aw, let's just sit here a few more minutes. Please?"

He looked to see his father nodding. "Okay, but just a few."

It was obvious his father had the same feeling that he did about this place.

Ethan fell back on the rock and enjoyed the sun's warmth filtering through a huge old overhanging cottonwood tree. "Ya know, Daddy, this is my favorite place in the whole world. God sure musta been feelin' good the day he created it."

Sid glanced at him then inspected the pristine setting. "Yep, I'm sure it was a cut above his average day while creating the universe."

"I think I'll just make this my special place forever."

His daddy didn't respond. Ethan noticed he stared expressionless, but finally did flutter his eyelids and looked down at Ethan, as if seeing him for the first time. Silence lingered.

Ethan thought his daddy appeared a bit strange. He sat up. "Somethin' wrong?"

A cardinal, winging by interrupted Sid's bland gaze. His eyes picked up the bird and followed it until it became a small red dot far down the creek channel. "Not really. It's just that your Uncle Ben said that very same thing when he was about your age."

Ethan couldn't remember ever seeing his father talk about his older brother without becoming sad. "I wish I'd known him."

"I wish you could've known him, but…"

"But what?"

"I'm not so sure I knew him very well either."

"I don't understand."

Sid held a thoughtful frown for a moment. "I suppose that makes two of us."

Ethan wrinkled his nose. "Huh?"

His father heaved a sigh. "Never mind. Come on, we'd better get back to the house or your momma'll beat both of us with a stick." He slid off into the water and dog-paddled to the other side. He slipped on his jeans and boots then wadded his socks and shoved them in his pocket. As he did, he looked at Ethan just coming out of the water. "You need a haircut."

Ethan shoved the plastered and splayed hair away from his eyes. "Aw, come on. Let's see how long it'll get before school starts."

"You really want to let it grow until September?" He began walking towards the tractor for the short ride up the hill.

Ethan trotted to catch up. "Yeah. Can I?"

Sid shrugged. "I can't think of a good reason why not. It is summer vacation after all." He climbed into the driver's seat.

"Do you think Momma'll mind?" Ethan asked then shinnied up onto the cultivator to stand on the toolbar behind his father.

Sid puffed out his chest. "Hey, we're the men of the house," he said with a catty snort.

"Oh boy." Ethan felt like a rebel. But a sudden afterthought wiped the smile from his face. "Jessie's gonna be real mad that you're lettin' me do it, ya know."

Grinding the tractor into gear, it lurched forward. "You're probably right, but let me handle your sister." Engaging the hydraulic power lift, the cultivator rose to its highest position as Ethan held tighter to his father's shoulders from behind. "She's reached that God-awful age of believing she's blessed with twenty-twenty vision in all things."

"What does that mean?"

"It means she sees all and knows all with absolute clarity. She thinks inhabitants of planet earth should all wear bifocals so they can see things clearly. You know, like she does." He turned to Ethan and laughed then throttled up the big green tractor. The diesel engine screamed its response. With a jerk, they took off and bounced along the turn-row that followed the contours of the cotton rows. "Hang on tight," he shouted then pushed the throttle full open. The tractor roared, quickly attaining full speed of less than twenty miles-per-hour.

Ethan imagined it to be a chariot pulled along the banks of the Nile with a team of four perfectly matched white stallions. Up and over a series of erosion control terraces thrilled him. He whooped and hollered all the way.

As Sid drove the tractor to the overhead diesel tank behind the house and parked, Faye poked an arm out from behind the screen door, waving a kitchen towel--the signal for suppertime.

Ethan waved back. He rode the cultivator to the ground as his father released the hydraulics. A turn of the key and the tractor went silent--a country kind of silence. Ethan swatted at a sweat bee he heard coming his direction long before it arrived to perch on his ear. He leaped from his chariot to the ground. A skittish hen took flight with a squawk only to land a few feet away and again scratch for things to eat in the Texas soil. "We're comin', Momma," he shouted and ran the few feet to the back porch.

After a quick inspection, Faye noticed his partially dried and unruly hair swept back from the windy tractor ride. "You're a ragamuffin, ya know that?" She tried to flatten his hair to his head, but up and out was the only way it'd go. "We've got to get you into Plainfield sometime this week for a haircut."

"About that," Sid said, joining them, "Ethan wanted to let it grow until school started." He pushed out his lower lip. "I couldn't see any harm in it."

"That's over two months!" Faye waved it off as silly and headed back to the kitchen. "I don't think that's a good idea at all. For heaven's sake, he'll be wearing it in a ponytail." She tossed the small towel onto the countertop with a force Ethan recognized as his mother's way of ending a conversation.

Ethan followed close behind holding his hands clasped together and pleading, "Come on, Momma. Please. It's only hair."

Jessie marched down the hall into the kitchen and confronted her mother. "If you let that little goofball grow his hair all summer, then I think it's only fair you let me date."

"Whoa. Hang on a danged minute," Sid said, pushing his way to the front of the line. "You're only fourteen and dating is not even in the same ballpark as growing hair."

"That's not fair!" She locked crossed arms over her chest.

"Don't raise your voice to your father like that," Faye snapped. "Besides, your daddy and I haven't agreed to allow Ethan to do that anyway. It's a frivolous idea and certainly not a cinch."

"What?" Ethan slapped his sides. "But Daddy already told me--"

9

"Hush up!" She held a stern finger to the tip of his nose. "Ya hear?"

A smile crept across Jessie's face as her smug nose turned upward.

"But Momma, she only said that to keep me from--"

"I said hush!"

His lip quivered. He looked to his father for support. It didn't come. He ran, throwing open the screen door, allowing it to slam on the way out.

"Be back before dark, Ethan," his father called out, as if nothing at all was wrong.

Daddy should be begging for my doggone forgiveness. He kept looking over his shoulder, wondering why his father wasn't chasing after him to apologize for betraying him like that.

Ethan retraced the path of the tractor ride home down the hill over the terraces all the way to the bend in the creek. He swam across and climbed to the higher rock then dropped and dangled his feet over the edge. He picked up pebbles and hurled them at the water's surface--bitterness propelling each one.

Jessie always gets her way! He threw another rock at a cottonwood tree. The impact sent a sparrow searching for safer haven. Tears blurred his vision. He held his breath, forcing blood into his face then exploded, "It's not fair!" he shouted. His voice echoed down the creek channel.

"You're right. It's not fair," came a voice from somewhere to his side.

Startled, Ethan's darting gaze scanned the tree line but saw nothing. "Who's there?"

"A friend."

Failing to spot the source of the voice, "This is private property. You shouldn't be here." Ethan looked all about.

"I know. It's been in the Lee family since your great-great grandfather Mitchell Lee homesteaded this little piece of heaven at the end of the Civil War."

"How do you know that? And, where the heck are you?" Movement caught his eye in a place he'd already looked several times.

A young man walked from between two cottonwood trees. "I'm right here."

"Whew," Ethan said, pretending to wipe sweat from his forehead. "I thought for a second you might be a ghost."

"Would that scare you, seeing a ghost I mean?"

"Well, yeah! That's a dumb question."

"I know what you mean. Just the word "ghost" is enough to raise the hair on my arms."

Ethan studied the young man, unable to take his eyes away as he approached. He felt comfortable with the stranger's presence. "Do you live around here?"

"Yep, all my life." He came to stand over Ethan. "May I sit by you?"

"Sure, I guess so." He pitched another stone into the water. "If you've always lived around here, how come I've never seen you before?"

"You have. You just don't remember."

Ethan examined the young man's face. "I have seen you before…somewhere. Do you live at the Bradley's?"

"Nope."

"I didn't think so. Besides, that's over a mile from here." He swept his hand across the stone surface he sat on, pushing small twigs into the water. "Even if you did live there, I don't think you'd walk all this way just to sit on a rock and visit with me. But where do you live?"

"For now I think I'll just tell you I live right here on this bend in Meandering Creek. If I tried to give you directions where I came from, it'd confuse you."

"You are from Texas, aren't you?"

"Certainly. Where else? This is the greatest state in the union. And, speaking of great places," he fanned his arms wide, "this is such a wonderful place right here, don't you think?"

Drawing a deep breath, "Yeah, it's neat." He leaned back on his elbows.

The young man emulated Ethan's posture. "I bet God was feeling pretty good the day he created it."

Ethan sat bolt upright. "Hey, I told my daddy that very same thing a while ago." He looked the young man in the eyes and tried to remember where he'd seen him. "Maybe I've seen you on the streets in Plainfield."

"Not likely," the young man said, as he flicked a twig into the air and watched the breeze carry it to the water below.

Ethan tilted his head. "You don't say a whole lot, do you?"

"Sure, when I have something that needs sayin'."

"And when would that be?"

"How about now?"

"Ethan chuckled. "What's the deal, you waitin' for an invitation?"

The young man nodded. "Sort of. I'm not the type to rattle on unless someone's willing to listen. Are you willing to hear what I have to say?"

"Heck, I'm only ten years old, goin' on eleven, and no one ever asks my opinion about anything. I'm usually beggin' to say something." He leaped to his feet, pacing behind the young man, hands draped on his hips above the drooping blue jean cut-offs, and taking long exaggerated steps. Water dripped from the ragged denim fringes. He placed a finger to his lips and tapped them as an academic with profound thoughts might. "You have my permission to speak. What's on your mind?"

"Don't be too hard on your dad. Okay?"

Ethan stopped pacing so fast he almost fell forward. He became confused and dropped back to again sit next to the young man. "Whaddaya mean?"

He flicked his chin toward the house. "I mean Sid had a reason for not pushing your case up there. He didn't want to pit you against your sister over something as unimportant as letting your hair grow." As the young man waited for a response, he sent a flat stone skipping across the creek to land in the mud on the other side.

"How do you know this stuff?"

"Let me just say that if giving you directions where I came from would confuse you, then telling you how I know these things would really make your head spin. The young man rose. "But I do need to beg your trust and ask you not to tell your family about me. If you do, they'll demand to know who I am and it'd only embarrass you."

"Why?"

"Because I can't talk to them."

"Why not?"

"It's simple. As rude as it may sound, you're the only one allowed to see and talk to me. Sorry. That's just the way it is."

"You're right, that is rude," Ethan said as a thought struck him. His eyes grew large and then scooted back until the chinaberry tree behind him stopped his retreat. "You *are* a ghost."

The young man didn't move or even blink. He held a smile and waited.

"If you're not, then how come I can see and hear you but they can't?"

"Have you ever heard of the age of innocence?"

"No."

"Let me see if I can explain it." He effortlessly rose to his feet and stepped over to the nearest chinaberry sapling. He walked full circle around it until he again faced Ethan. "We're all born with a straightforward unbiased view of the universe."

"Unbiased?"

"That just means you see everything in clear-cut ways. You haven't reached an age where decision-making is difficult."

"Oh."

"Got it?"

"I think so."

"In the first stages of life when we first become aware of the world around us, we don't judge others. In fact, we're incapable of it." He grinned. "Not enough stored information in our little cue-ball brains.

"What's a cue ball?"

"Never mind. The important thing is, we're born believing and accepting of everyone for what and who they are, everyone is equal, no debate. We believe that dividing lines are plain, black and white, yes or no, but no gray areas. As we grow older, temptations and problems start weaseling in. We begin to see more of those gray areas in need of interpretation before we act."

"What's a gray area?"

"Not black, not white, but gray...between yes and no; something that's not quite right but not quite wrong either."

"Really?"

"Sure. The number of temptations and choices--gray areas--begins to overload our ability to decide. That blurs the line between right and wrong. Eventually, we all leave the age of innocence. Sharp intuitive sensitivities disappear, along with that unbiased view of the world. It's unfortunate really." He took another swing around the chinaberry sapling. "Regrettably for some, hardened criminals for example, *all* sensitivities vanish." He paused. "You don't have to worry about that. The young man again sat beside Ethan. "But, there will come a time you'll be less sensitive to experiencing...well, me for example. You're not there yet. Therefore, I have the great privilege of coming to see you."

Ethan sighed. "I didn't understand a thing you told me."

"Then not telling you where I came from or how I knew those things was the right decision." He patted Ethan on the back and rose. He stepped over to the big cottonwood tree and leaned against it. A breeze rustled the topmost leaves. "Ethan, would you like to kiss a girl or have a girl kiss you?"

"Oh ick, no way; I don't want to swap spit with a girl. Good grief!"

"When you do, then the age of innocence will be more in your past than your present and certainly not in your future. Does that make it easier to understand?"

Ethan wrinkled his nose. "No." He dropped a leaf and watched it drift to the water's surface. He then jerked his head toward the young man. "Are you messin' with me?"

The young man ignored the question. "One more thing; ask your dad about crop hail insurance." He stepped back and turned to walk away. "Your dad loves you but there are certain things he can't bring himself to do for fear of alienating your sister or you. It saddens me, but I may have had something to do with that way of thinking."

"Huh? Alienating? What does that mean?" Ethan scratched his head. He tossed a handful of rock chips at the water and thought about all the things he'd just been told. He glanced over his shoulder for an answer but the young man was nowhere to be seen. "Wait a minute. Don't go. I still have questions."

A fading voice floated in on the breeze, "All in good time, Ethan."

Chapter Three

Sid offered Ethan an apologetic glance as he grasped the top of the steering wheel with both hands. "I suppose I can still make it happen … if that's what you really want. After all, I did promise."

The pickup truck bounced over a shallow washout in the dirt road as Ethan chose to stare at the passing telephone line poles rather than face his daddy. There was the unmistakable tinge of uneasiness in his father's words. If he took his father's offer, things might get nasty at home. "Nah," he finally said. "Like I said the other day, 'it's only hair'. I think I'll wait until something comes along that I really want. Then it'll be worth making Jessie mad." He pushed out his lower lip and nodded then grinned as he remembered all those times he'd made his sister angry simply because he could. "I can wait."

His father relaxed and shoved the bill of his cap up until it rested on the back of his head. "That certainly makes my job easier." Sid steered the truck onto the blacktop toward Plainfield. "Now, since Jessie thought she was so darned clever by hinging dating on the length of your hair, she has no argument." He drew a satisfied breath and turned full attention to the highway ahead. "If you really want to get her, you can tell her it was our little plan all along to keep her from dating."

"Yeah," he said, drawing out the word. "Cool idea."

"But, just toss it out there one time. Don't torment her with it?"

"Dad, is there such a thing as ghosts?"

15

"Huh? Where in the world did that come from? How did we get from ways to make your sister angry to ghosts?"

"I dunno; just curious. Is there?"

His daddy scratched the day-old whisker stubble on his chin. The time he remained silent indicated serious consideration. Finally, "Well, it's certainly a topic that's been debated and argued for centuries but I think all the evidence has been anecdotal and there's been no empirical evidence to support it."

"I suppose since you're using words I don't understand that means you don't have a clue."

"You're pretty smart, hotshot."

Ethan shrugged and nodded, "I think so...sometimes." He looked and saw a thunderstorm beginning to tower in the distance in an otherwise clear early afternoon sky. "Other times I don't feel smart a'tall. There's way too much I don't understand."

"Son, do you know what the difference is between an intelligent person and one that might not be the sharpest tool in the shed?"

"What?"

"Intelligent people ask questions...lots of questions. They don't care if people think it's amusing that they don't understand something. Their desire to know overrides all that other stuff. Dimmer bulbs have no curiosity; they don't ask questions."

While watching that thunderstorm billowing in the distance, he remembered something then suddenly realized it had gone quiet. He looked and saw that his father waited for a response. "Oh yeah, sure, that makes sense."

"So, buddy, you just keep on asking."

"Okay." The distant storm looked out of place in an otherwise cloudless sky and that made him think about the young man at the creek and the conversation they'd had. "Daddy, what's crop hail insurance? Is that a way to keep it from hailing?"

Sid laughed. "When I told you to keep asking questions, I had no idea the odd assortment I'd be getting." They passed the Plainfield city limit sign, next to the Bower County Grain Elevator. "Having hail insurance can't keep it from hailing, but if it does come and damages or destroys a crop, it'll provide some measure of reimbursement for the damage to the farmer who owns it."

"Do we have it on our cotton crop?"

"No, son, we don't. The way I see it, it's so darned expensive that the one time it might pay to have it, after several good crop years, the premium cost over that period of time would probably exceed the loss of a single cotton crop." Sid drew his brow down to a curious slant. "But you know what? We haven't had hail damage in years. It's strange the subject is coming up now."

Ethan wondered what good he did by asking such a simple question, aside from putting the notion on his daddy's mind.

His daddy eased the pickup truck into an angle parking space in front of Main Street Barber Shop. Slipping the vehicle into park, He sat unmoving, staring at something straight ahead. It appeared as though he might be lost in a thought.

"Since I'm not going to let my hair grow long, how about I go the other way and have it all buzzed off?" He threw open the door.

It took his daddy a second or so to realize the question had been directed at him. "Huh? Oh, sure, I think that's a great idea. You'd hate messin' with long hair anyhow." Throwing open the door, he got out. "Come on, let's get 'er done."

The chairs along one wall were nearly filled with men waiting their turn. Fritz Bucher, a burly but nice old German-American in faded bib overalls extended a friendly hand toward his daddy. He farmed just south of town. A few of Fritz's teeth were missing; so, the smile that came with the offer of a handshake appeared comical. His daddy took a giant step and heartily accepted Fritz's hand. The old guy moved down a chair to create two seats. "Y'all have a seat."

As expected, the general buzz was about farming and crops. Ethan heard a man down the line say, "I just came from Tremble's Insurance. My gut was telling me to buy crop insurance." The youngster looked to his father, instantly drawn into the conversation, as old Mr. Bucher said, "I read in the Farmer's Almanac that July in the Rolling Plains is going to be especially stormy this year." His German accent had not entirely gone away.

"Fritz, isn't crop insurance this late in the season pretty darned expensive?" His daddy asked. "I mean we are past planting deadline."

Ethan leaned close and whispered, "You mean there's someone who says when we have to stop planting every year?"

Old Mr. Bucher burst into a bellowing laugh. His belly bounced inside his faded overalls.

Ethan's face reddened, not realizing he'd been overheard.

Sid put his arm around him. "It's okay."

Ethan dropped his head, embarrassed.

Fritz, still laughing, messed Ethan's hair with a swipe. "You'll learn to be a farmer yet."

Sid explained, "The deadline has to do with the length of the growing season. If we don't have cotton planted by the middle of June, the rule of thumb is that it probably won't mature before a killing freeze stops the growth cycle in the fall. Should that happen, unopened bolls would be worthless and the cotton lost." He turned back to Fritz. "And, once we passed the fifteenth of June I was thinking the premium for crop insurance would probably go up fast."

"He's right," Fritz told Ethan. The old man looked back at Sid. "But this year I'm going with the Almanac and taking the chance."

"Well, you've given me some serious thinking to do," Sid said, as he peered through the front window of the shop, beyond the passing traffic across Main Street to the sign painted on the window of Tremble's Insurance. "It's funny how things work out sometimes," he said to no one in particular. "I hadn't given it any thought until you ask about it, Ethan. Now, I find out it's the topic of the day at the barbershop."

The flash of enlightenment suddenly struck him. Ethan now understood why the young man at the creek urged him to ask his father about insurance. But, even as that question found an answer, many more were created. *Why would the guy even care? And, why'd he tell me to ask it?*

One of the three barbers signaled Ethan to his chair.

He jumped to his feet, took a step then stopped and turned. "Daddy, is it okay if I go swimmin' this afternoon?"

"Sure, as long as you do your chores first."

He climbed into the chair; the barber pumped it higher with his foot then snapped the loose hair from a cape and let it drift down over Ethan's body, fastening it at the neck. "Buzz it," Ethan said with authority. "I don't want to be back in here until it's time for school to start." He appreciated the sweet smell of talcum powder and various bottles of hair treatments that lined the shelf in front of the mirror. The humming electric clippers touched his forehead and plowed a furrow all the way to the back of his head, hair falling in clumps.

Meanwhile, his thoughts rested elsewhere, painting a picture of his domain, the bend in Meandering Creek, wondering if the young man would be there later. He wanted to understand more about the guy; what his deal was, where he'd come from and where he went to. Ethan's curiosity about the stranger had suddenly taken over.

With every pass of the clippers, Ethan felt coolness on his head he hadn't known before and would've sworn on a bible there was a breeze inside the barbershop. The haircut, from beginning to end, lasted less than a minute. He reached from beneath his cape and felt stiff stubble on his head. The barber spun him around to look at the result in the mirror. Amazed, he examined the pasty white of his head, compared to the deep tan of his face. *I wonder if my new friend will even recognize me?* Suddenly, he became uneasy that he might not see him today; worse yet, ever again. Premature affection for the stranger was just one more on a growing list of mysteries. *For Pete's sake, I don't even know the guy. Why do I care?*

Chapter Four

Clearly, Ethan's momma wanted to shout and it was also plain as day that her best effort might fail. "You spent over two-thousand dollars on it?"

His daddy put gentle hands on her shoulders and guided her backward to lean against the kitchen counter. "Settle down, honey. It wasn't a spur-of-the-moment decision…not exactly."

"Oh really." Anger still threatened to boil over, her voice remaining higher than usual. "Well, if it wasn't part of the business plan when you left after dinner, at what point did this *carefully* considered idea to buy expensive crop insurance occur to you?" She parked hands on hips, tapping an angry foot, waiting impatiently for an answer.

Ethan watched his daddy try again to calm her, all the while cozy in the notion that he was merely an innocent bystander. Sid's second attempt failed too. While watching his mother seethe, he thought, *I wish I could tell you who told me to ask Daddy about that.* He noticed that he'd become the target of Sid's searching eyes. That's when it occurred to him that his father might just do that; ask why the question came up to begin with. *Oh, please, no, Daddy. Don't ask me.* Now concerned that he might be put in an awkward situation, one in which he might be forced to lie, he shrank away from the argument. Curiosity, though, kept him within hearing distance. He went no farther than around the corner and listened from the hallway safely out of sight.

His daddy tried several ways to explain the impulsive decision. But, it appeared that, to his momma, an admission of piddling away valuable cash would be the only acceptable response. His momma acted like a cornered mountain lion, money in that savings account, her cub. So she pressed for the only thing left to go after, full disclosure of foolishness. The cash in that account had been earmarked for a new pickup truck. The insurance purchase made acquiring a new truck unlikely.

"It came about innocently enough," Sid told her. "Ethan heard about hail insurance…somewhere and asked what it was for. I explained it to him on the way to town and. I'll be darn, if that wasn't the topic of conversation at the barbershop. Hon, it just kinda got me ta thinkin', that's all. It has been a long time since we've had a hailstorm. Don't you think the odds are beginning to stack against us?"

Not letting it go, she threw it back, "So, now you're a gambler?" That retort was the loudest and most pointed, so far.

Ethan peeked around the corner into the kitchen and saw his father stiffen. *He's gonna blow.*

"Yeah, ever since I decided to make farming my life!"

Then Ethan saw the unthinkable. Sister Jessie walked right past him, saying nothing, turned the corner into the kitchen and pulled a chair in close so she could listen to the heated exchange like it was a ringside seat at a boxing match. A catty look of satisfaction came over her. She clearly relished not being the brunt of their anger.

It irked Ethan. *She thinks she's the center of the doggone universe.* She glanced to him repeatedly with that stupid look on her face. He frowned, hoping she'd take the hint and go away. She didn't--just kept grinning, clearly amused. *Idiot!*

Ethan figured it was time to get out of the house. His daddy had his hands full with his angry momma. He didn't want to be around if Jessie should toss gasoline on the fire by making some crack worthy of that idiotic expression.

As debate continued over that two-thousand-and-six-dollar trip to the barbershop, Ethan slipped out through the back door, careful not to let the screen door slam this time. He wanted no attention, quietly slipping away.

The sun beamed hot. Super-short hair let rays land directly on his white pate. As soon as he cleared the gate at the back yard fence, six chickens fought for a place at his heels. He didn't notice, wondering instead if the stranger would be at the creek. The chickens broke rank one by one, as each discovered nothing tasty would be forthcoming.

Walking down a row of waist-high cotton plants, he absently brushed open palms over the tops of them, like small airplanes flying over treetops. Concern over the argument still blazing up at the house faded as distance from it increased. The prospect of diving into cool water seemed extra inviting.

Breaking through the thicket of chinaberry saplings, he straightened and looked with reverence for a moment at the sight. Drawing a deep breath, he sighed satisfaction.

"You're right. There isn't a finer place, on earth anywhere," came the voice.

Startled, Ethan's breath hitched. He spun around, looking for the origin of the comment. "Hey, I didn't say that out loud." He stopped to think. "Did I?" He turned one more circle, trying to see the source of the familiar voice and, there, on the lower of the two jutting rocks overhanging the creek, sat the young man. Ethan would've sworn that he'd already looked there. In fact, he thought he checked there first.

"No, it wasn't audible in the usual sense, but you thought it so loud I heard it."

"You must take me for a real dipwad." He grinned and hoped the stranger would smile along with him for figuring out the joke so quickly.

But the stranger remained expressionless.

After a moment, "Okay, then I don't understand," Ethan said.

"Come on over and sit."

"I think I'll dive in and stay in the water, if it's okay with you. It's hot today." He jumped from the bank into the water and swam across to the young man, holding on to the rock where he sat. He continued bobbing and whirling around, reveling in the coolness. He looked at the young man's face and saw that his skin seemed perfectly dry. "How come you're not sweating? It's hot out here! There's not even a breeze."

"I've learned tolerance to temperature variances. The summer heat doesn't bother me, nor does cold in winter."

"Oh, okay," he said, even though it wasn't really an answer. He had more pressing things to know. "You never did tell me if you were a ghost or not. Are you?" He turned loose from the rock and swam in a tight circle on his back.

"I've already answered that question. I said *ghost* is a scary word and *friend* is not. So, I'm your friend."

"But, what about--"

"I'll tell you what, touch my leg."

Ethan swam around and bobbed in front of him as the stranger took off his old-fashioned shoes and socks, rolled up his pant legs and dropped his bare feet into the water.

Ethan moved to within inches of an exposed leg, examined it, then took a probing poke at it below the knee, then again, and again, finally hitting the young man's leg with a doubled fist.

"Ow! I hope you don't make a habit of hitting people like that." He massaged the point of impact.

Ethan smiled sheepishly. "No. But sometimes I sure would like to wallop my sister."

"Your sister is in the process of changing from child to adult, from girl to woman. Her mind is torn between two worlds. You'll be there soon too."

"So, now you think I'm going to change into a woman?

The young man grinned. "No."

Ethan dipped below the surface, took in a mouthful of water then spewed a geyser from between circled lips.

"No, you'll always be an all-American male, but you'll have struggles as you grow from the boy you are now into manhood. That's why I'm telling you to be tolerant of Jessie's craziness."

Ethan climbed from the water to sit next to him. "What does tolerant mean anyway? I should just put up with her crap?"

"Hey, you shouldn't be using words like that." The young man sighed. "It simply means you shouldn't respond in-kind. It'll pass."

"Do I really have a choice?"

"Sure." He flicked a dried chinaberry into the water. "There's always a choice. In this case, tolerance would be the right one...my opinion, of course. But, it's your decision; I'm only suggesting it as the better alternative."

A shadow moved across and Ethan looked up to see a single cumulus cloud beginning to lift with daytime heating. "I asked about hail insurance, like you said, but it only cost a lot of money and caused an argument between Momma and Daddy." He looked into the young man's face and quickly added, "Hey, I know where I've seen you before. You worked at the Bower County Grain Elevator last summer."

"Nope, sorry," the young man said. "Don't worry about the tiff between your parents. It'll be okay." He pulled his bare feet from the water and rose effortlessly, without using his hands. He then picked up his shoes and socks.

"Hey, how'd you do that?"

"It's a trick I learned, a simple matter of balance really."

Ethan looked to the stranger's feet and saw no water on them and no wet footprints on the rock. "How come you're not wet?"

"Remember the old saying, 'like water off a duck's back'?"

"Yeah. So?"

"There you go. It's just like water off a duck's back."

"Can I do that?"

"I don't know. Give it a try."

Ethan dipped his feet in the water and then jumped up to watch water roll from his lower leg, over his feet, pooling on the rock around them. "It didn't work." He looked around. "Hey, where'd you go?"

"I'll be back," came the voice. "In the meantime, I want you to remember something: This is not a normal crop season and there'll be time to re-plant cotton this year."

"Whaddaya mean by that?" Ethan turned around and around trying to spot him. "Wait a minute. I don't understand."

No answer.

"Please don't go," he shouted. He heard nothing but his echo coming back and the rustle of leaves in the trees. Finally, he gave up and muttered,

"How can he answer all my questions and I still don't know anything; then all of a sudden, poof! He disappears?"

He noticed passing shadows increasing and saw that clouds had begun to cluster and the sky darken.

Ethan decided it was pointless to walk all the way to the creek without swimming. He dove in and swam down to see if his old friend the catfish was still in his hole. And there the critter was looking back at him. He gingerly reached in and touched it on the snout. It backed deeper into the crack in the rock. As he held his breath and watched the big old fish, he thought: *Why would I need to know if there'd be time to re-plant?* He watched the rhythmic movements of the fish's mouth, as if Mr. Catfish might be trying to give him an answer. It had become a comfort to see the old guy in his hole every day. He swam to the surface.

As soon as Ethan came up, a particularly hard gust of wind sent leaves and loose debris off the rocks down into his face. Spitting grit, he washed it out, noticing the wind had cooled. He shivered. The sky had become totally overcast. The tall cottonwood and chinaberry trees prevented him from seeing the whole picture. He thought he heard a voice and cocked an ear homeward. Sure enough, momma called for him.

He ran to open ground beyond the trees and waved to her. Then, he saw why the air had cooled and the wind had abruptly picked up. A massive thunderhead blotted out the sun. Lightning flashed in feathery fingers from cloud to cloud. He fantasized a big gray monster wearing a crown made of lightning bolts. He gazed in awe at the beast of his imagination still unfolding and coming to life. Coolness had nothing to do with the shiver this time. He picked his way carefully over the rough, hard surface of the turn-row into the softer plowed ground of the cotton rows then sprinted.

As he ran, he saw his father herd an old mother cow and her calf into the barn while holding that green John Deere cap to his head against the gusting wind. Dust and sand lifted and streamed just above the surface as if it had a slithering life of its own. Chickens ran and flew then crowded and fought to get through the entrance into the safer haven of their coop.

He glanced back and saw the Bradley's house disappear behind a rain shield. That was about a mile. A brilliant flash blinded him, followed by a ground-shaking boom. His sprint had suddenly gained even more speed.

His daddy hollered for him to hurry and get to the house. He needed no encouragement, meeting him at the back screen door. Faye and Jessie stood on the other side urging them in.

As strong-willed and opinionated as his momma could be at times, storms scared her. She transformed from self-confident debater of family politics to the equivalent of a whimpering child. In the confusion, Ethan noticed how short his momma actually was. By next summer, he figured he'd be as tall. She hugged his sister so tight he thought it might suffocate Jessie. But, it wasn't really a hug, more like taking refuge from fear. With each clap of thunder, she jerked Jessie closer and tighter.

Even before his breathing evened out, the rain started; drops big enough to explode into smaller ones on the back porch landed with audible splats. Sid pulled Ethan away from the door to shut out the storm, separating nature's chaos from the safety within. Just before he closed it, he glanced skyward. "Oh my god."

"What is it?" Faye squealed.

"Rotation in the cloud."

Faye pulled Jessie to an interior hallway and both slid down the wall to sit it out.

Ethan hung tight to his father as he moved to a window for a better look. His father seemed fascinated. Sid began babbling an eyewitness account. "The storm is moving fast…forty, maybe fifty miles an hour. If we're lucky, it'll pass before reaching full potential." He spoke loud enough for Faye and Jessie to hear in the hallway. Moving from window to window, Sid froze once he made it to the small window over the kitchen sink. "Ethan come here and look at this!" He pointed upward through the window. "This could be a once-in-a-lifetime event for you to witness."

Ethan watched rotating clouds tighten, and then a narrow tail descended from its center, coming down in slow motion from the mother cloud. He had never seen a real tornado before. Becoming scared, he stepped closer to his father--near enough their bodies touched. He swallowed hard, yet unable to take his eyes from it. High on the tips of his toes, he gawked through the kitchen window as long as he could make it out.

"The funnel is moving fast. It shouldn't hit us. If it touches ground it'll be several miles away and moving away." The relief in his father's voice was evident.

The announcement didn't inspire confidence in his mother or sister. They clung to one another, huddled on the floor down the hall adjacent to the kitchen. The tornado may have missed them, but a dangerous thunderstorm with strong wind raged outside.

Ethan had become more curious than afraid, as he watched the rope-like tail move in a slow undulation, elongating toward the ground. He could tell the moment contact was made. The force churned dirt and debris at its base. Set against the multi-toned gray backdrop, it looked like the writhing tail of a dragon trying to climb a slippery rock face, sliding backwards to the ground. His mouth hung loose. His heart pounded.

And then the rain set in. The funnel disappeared in it. Ethan wanted to keep it in sight but couldn't. The rain blew at a stiff angle. He couldn't see beyond the backyard. Embedded within the roar of torrential rain hitting the roof was an occasional thunk that sounded out of place. "What's that, Daddy?" he shouted above the noise.

Sid slammed a fist on the back door jamb. "It's hail." The sound on the roof changed dramatically. Besides the roar of rain, the sound of hundreds of hammers hit simultaneously. Suddenly a loud crash was the odd sound. A kitchen window shattered.

Ethan turned to see a chunk of ice the size of a baseball slide across the floor, chased by shards of glass.

"Get away from the windows!" Sid yelled then ran to the bedroom. He returned with a bedspread in his hand then held it clumsily over the broken window. "Ethan, give me a hand, but watch out for the glass."

Sid held one side and Ethan the other. It became heavy, saturated by driving rain. An occasional thwump-thwump sound of hailstones hit the wet cloth. Water pooled around Ethan's feet, streaming in all directions over the floor and across the kitchen. They had no choice but hold on until the storm moved past.

Ethan's muscles ached from holding the wet bedspread high over his head. The rain and hail stopped abruptly. Cautiously, he let down his end of the bedspread then ran to the other window to see if the funnel was again visible. It was, doing a slow motion dance in the distance but now had begun retreating to the mother cloud.

Sid followed and looked over Ethan's shoulder. "It probably didn't damage more than fences and, maybe, Harvey Tucker's old barn. But that was about to collapse anyway."

Faye and Jessie still held one another but now on their feet and taking tentative steps toward the kitchen. Faye's strong personality returned. Strangely, that comforted him. "Ethan, get to your bedroom and put shoes on before you slice your feet open." Although the order was firm, he detected embarrassment. *Feelin' a little silly, Momma?* He swelled with pride at his courage in the face of nature's anger.

After he'd slipped into his favorite sneakers and returned, he looked through the open back door beyond the screen door. His father stood on the porch. It appeared as though a heavy weight pressed down on his shoulders, rounding them. He walked past Jessie and Faye, who'd begun sweeping up glass and mopping water from the floor. "What is it, Daddy? What do you see?"

Sid sighed, moaned then made a sound like he was about to cry. "I see a lot of work and money down the drain."

Ethan joined his father on the porch and cautiously looked up at him, uncertain if what he saw on his father's face were tears or raindrops. Only then did he follow his father's eyes.

It reminded him of a lawn where a mower had taken a pass in tall grass, except it had to be a mile wide. Even the trees along the creek had been stripped bare. Cotton stalks littered the ground like green confetti. He knew the crop was lost. The unseen force that crushed his father's spirit spilled over onto him. Sadness slumped his shoulders too.

Chapter Five

Ethan climbed the ladder, squinting into the morning sun as it appeared over the rooftop. He clutched a bound bundle of wooden shingles. Reaching the roof's edge, his eyes were drawn to gaping holes surrounded by splintered wood. His father had told him it had to be repaired quickly before it rained again or next time the damage would be inside and not just on the roof. He grunted and heaved the bundle near to where his father sat nailing a shingle between his splayed legs.

"Thanks, hotshot. But keep 'em comin'. It'll take the better part of the day just to get the broken ones replaced."

After Ethan delivered up another bundle, his father paused for a break, letting the hammer lay in his gloved hand at his side, flicking sweat from his nose with the other, expression stoic with a set jaw. He scanned the cotton field beyond the yard. From the rooftop, the extent of devastation was stark. His father went back to replacing shingles, obviously not wanting to think about that problem while the roof still needed repairing. But he did sneak glances between every nail he drove.

Compelled to put a voice to what he assumed his father thought, "How long will it be before you can get the tractor back in the field?"

"Two...maybe three days; anytime before that and it'd probably sink up to the axle in those low areas where water is standing..." Sid used his hammer pointing out potential trouble spots across the mud slickened field. "...Like there and that one over there."

Ethan sat on the edge of the roof and looked across the farm. His feet dangled high above the grass of the backyard, still glistening with morning dew.

"Be careful. The roof is the only damage I want to deal with today."

"Okay." He scooted back from the edge until his legs lay flat. "Ya know, two or three days isn't long. Are you going to replant?"

His father glanced at him while positioning another shingle. "That's what I'm wondering right now." He placed a nail and pounded it in. "I'm not sure we have enough of the growing season left."

"How about the insurance, will that help?"

Hammer held high, Sid abruptly stopped. A less serious look came over him. He dropped the hammer and pulled his gloves off and sat back, pulling his knees up and draping his hands over them. "I guess it will."

"Does that mean there's no reason to replant?"

"Maybe...then again, maybe not."

"Won't it pay for the damage?"

"Sort of; it'll pay up to a set amount per acre. It'll justify the expense of the premium for sure. Unfortunately, even if we draw the maximum settlement, it'd only amount to about sixty-percent of what the cotton would've fetched at harvest."

"Oh," Ethan said, suddenly understanding what the young man at the creek had told him. "In that case, I have a strong feeling there'll be time to replant. This year's going to be a different kind of year."

Sid's eyebrows shot up. He drew a half-grin. "Think so, huh? And just why is that?"

He shrugged. "Just a feeling."

"Well, I hate to strip what little meat there is on your bony little hunch, but do you realize a killing frost would have to be at least a whole month later than usual for a second planting to make it this season?" He put his gloves back on.

"Oh, I didn't know it'd have to be that long..." His voice trailed and he paused then said, "...But I still say it's a different kind of year."

"I appreciate your enthusiasm, but I'm afraid it'd be too much to hope for." The resignation in his voice was strong. He fished in the canvas apron pouch tied to his waist for another nail.

"Didn't you tell Momma that the day you decided to become a farmer was also the day you became a gambler?"

"I didn't realize you heard that."

"It was kinda hard to miss. You said it pretty loud."

His father sighed. "I suppose I did." He maintained focus on the head of a nail.

"In that case, I still say there's time to replant."

"I was thinking about going back in with some type of fast maturing crop, like sorghum maybe, cut it green and bale it for hay. We'll need it for the cows come wintertime anyhow."

"Would it make as much money?"

"No, not nearly as much as a good cotton crop. but coupled with the insurance settlement we could possibly come out okay, maybe even ahead just a little. It's certainly safer than rolling the dice on another cotton crop."

"I still say replant the cotton. Just think what a great year it'd be? Make for a pretty darned good Christmas, I'd say." He grinned.

"You'd say that, would ya?"

"Sure. We'd be better off, right?"

"Yep, far better, but it'd be a huge risk." The lack of conviction in the statement seemed to indicate his daddy was thinking about taking the chance. "I don't know what makes you so sure of that and if anyone should find out I was making my farming decisions on the advice of a ten year old boy--"

"Goin' on eleven though."

"Yeah, goin' on eleven." His father sincerely smiled for the first time since he began working on the roof. "It still might be embarrassing."

"I won't tell anyone."

"Good to know." He set the hammer down and looked across the devastated crop. Maybe lucky lightning can strike twice," he mumbled.

"What does that mean?"

"It means I'd better go to Plainfield tomorrow and buy cotton seed."

~ * ~

Idleness had no place on the Lee farm. Every member of the family played a role in getting the second-chance crop planted as soon as possible. Ethan happily watched Jessie struggle to pull fifty-pound seed sacks from the bed of the pickup truck and drop them at intervals along the turn-row. They took turns pulling the sacks out. He seldom had the opportunity to see his sister huff and puff and sweat like that. He grinned, almost to the point of laughing aloud. *This is so cool.* His mother drove the truck no faster than they could walk as he and Jessie followed along behind spacing sacks to be handy for Sid to refill seed boxes on the planter as needed.

Ethan saw a dust cloud lazily boil around the tractor as Sid pulled the planter through muddy areas carefully, so as not to bog it down. The hail had beaten the ground so hard it left behind a thin, dry crusty veneer on the surface. A film of fine powdery dust set loosely on top going airborne with the slightest breeze; yet below that half-inch of hard crust, it remained muddy. Should the tractor stick, valuable time would be lost. Every precaution had to be taken to keep the planter moving.

Jessie whined, "My hands are chapped."

"Yeah, well you'd better keep working," Ethan said, "Or you'll be chappin' dad's butt and he'll be whippin' yours."

"Ethan, I heard that," his mother shouted from the pickup cab. "Watch your mouth. Talk like that will get your rear-end in trouble, not hers."

"Yes ma'am. Sorry." The apology came quick and easy but he refused to wipe the silly grin from his face.

He saw Jessie check to see if their mother was still looking. When she seemed certain they weren't being watched, she flipped a one-finger insult. "Serves you right, you little moron," she hissed.

Without consciously thinking of it, the word "tolerance" popped into his head. "I'm sorry…I guess. I shouldn't've said that."

Jessie's sneer vanished.

Ethan couldn't remember the last time he'd seen her face without it-- especially awake and around him.

"You're…sorry?" she stammered then stared. The girl was clearly dumbfounded.

"Yeah, I guess I am."

"That's better." She turned her nose skyward and made another attempt to speak, something catty most likely, but couldn't seem to get it out. She actually appeared speechless.

He glanced and saw her look at him, as if she thought he might be sick. *This tolerance stuff is okay.* He smiled then dragged out the last bag of seed and dropped it on the ground.

His mother braked to a stop and got out. "That's good for now." Shielding her eyes from the sun, she inspected the neat row of standing sacks extending several hundred yards back. "If your daddy gets all this in the ground, it'll be too dark by then to go on today. I need to get back up to the house to start supper anyhow."

"Thank God," Jessie said, as if she'd been tortured all day."

Ethan looked toward the house and started to climb into the back of the pickup for the ride home, but the lure of the creek in the opposite direction, down the hillside, was strong. "Momma, can I go to the creek and swim for a while?"

"I suppose so. But be home by sunset." She fixed a hard gaze on him. "Promise?"

"Okay." He turned and began trotting off. "Not a problem."

Jessie slid off the tailgate. "I wanna go too. It's hot out here."

Faye nodded. "Good idea. Now I don't have to worry about your brother being down there alone."

Ethan didn't care one way or the other, but it was his brotherly duty to roll his eyes and look perturbed. "Come on then." He ran, checking occasionally on his sister. She seemed content to stroll along. He ran over the newly planted rows, his feet only coming down on the beds thrown up between the furrows. The freshly turned earth felt good under his bare feet. When he reached the tree line bordering the creek, he hardly slowed, stripping his t-shirt over his head, zipping between the trees, down the incline then diving headfirst into the inviting coolness. The water still floated a layer of leaves and branches from the hailstorm earlier in the week.

The first order of business was to dive down and check on his old friend the catfish. Once he found the appropriate crack in the rock, there he was, suspended. The fish seemed to be waiting for something that, indeed, came in the form of a morsel drifting down in front of his snout. Ol' Mr. Catfish sucked it up so fast it seemed to vanish. *I'll bring stale bread next, buddy.*

He shot back to the surface. The coolness on his sunburned close-cropped head was exaggerated--cooler there than anywhere else on his body.

Jessie just then appeared at the water's edge near the row of trees bordering the channel. He saw her examine the surroundings. She wasn't a frequent visitor to the creek. "Can I wade over to that big flat rock?"

"Nope, too deep. You gotta swim."

"But I don't want to get my clothes wet."

"Sorry."

"Okay. I'll have to trust you. I'm going to take my clothes off and I want you to look the other way until I get in the water... all the way in the water. You promise?"

She reached for the buttons on her blouse and was about to open it when she saw that he stared only then realizing he hadn't promised anything.

"Swear it, Ethan. Raise your hand and swear you won't look."

Bobbing around in the water, his left hand broke the surface. Then loudly, "I swear not to look." He crossed his fingers of the other hand and whispered, "Unless I can see everything."

"What did you say?"

"Nothing." He swam to the low jutting rock and turned his back to her. He held the edge of the stone surface that was at eye level as he continued lazily kicking his legs beneath the surface. Feeling devious, he wondered how long he should wait before turning back. Obviously it had to be before she said it was okay to look, but how long he couldn't say. His heart thumped. He felt heat rising in his face. His breathing quickened. *On the count of three: One, two...*he took a deep breath and held it...*three.* Pushing off from the rock, he turned quickly to see his fourteen-year-old sister without a stitch of clothing on, preparing to step into the creek. His heart pounded. He'd never seen a naked girl before. He felt strange, having no idea what that feeling was.

"You little twerp! You lied to me!" She no longer checked her footing or seemed concerned by the water temperature. She dove quickly and clumsily. She surfaced and sputtered. "If I had a swimsuit on, I'd be choking the breath outa you right now."

Ethan snickered. "Sorry. I thought you'd already gotten in the water."

"Sure you did."

Ethan still felt heat in his face. He leaned backwards and slowly swam in a circle on his back. It crossed his mind he should be thanking her, not apologizing. Even though the thought was sincere, any bold out-of-place comment would get him into trouble with his momma and daddy. Jessie would tattle on him for sure. As it stood, she couldn't be certain if it was an accident or not and would probably let it pass.

He tried changing the subject and her mood. "Hey, would you like to see my friend that lives in a big crack below the diving rock?"

"What are you talking about?" Clearly, the level of trust in her little brother had just hit low ebb. Her expression told the story; she questioned his intentions, probably thinking he might have another trick to pull.

"It's a catfish...big 'un, too. Been down there all summer. Who knows...it may have lived there for years."

"Won't it come after me if I go snooping into its home?"

"Nah. I've been swimming down to pet him almost every day. He hardly even moves when I touch him anymore."

"You touch it?"

"We're old friends now. I bet if he had hands he'd shake mine."

"Yeah, right." She thought about it for a moment. "Well...okay. But you go first."

"Follow me." Taking a deep breath, he swam down and held onto the edge of the crack to keep from bobbing to the surface. He looked up to see Jessie swimming down. It occurred to him that she had no idea just how clear the water was. He waved her over.

She stared intently into the crack in the rock. When she caught sight of the big fish, she became captivated and studied the docile creature.

But Ethan stared at her, not the fish, unable to keep from examining the entire length of her body. Her gaze, meanwhile, remained on the fascinating sight of a fish that didn't appear to care whether she was there or not. She lightly touched its whiskers.

It spooked.

So did she and yanked her hand back.

Ethan's moment of leering lasted long enough that he had a brief lapse of where he was. Running short on oxygen, he inadvertently inhaled and sucked water into his lungs and choked. He shot to the surface and held tight to the jutting rock, gagging and fighting to draw a full breath, then coughed up water.

Jessie followed him up. As soon as she broke the surface, "Are you all right?"

Still coughing, "Yeah. I'll be fine. Just sucked in a little water, that's all."

"Maybe Momma was right. You shouldn't swim down here alone."

"Don't tell Momma and Daddy. Please?"

He saw it in her expression. She had something on him. The wry grin gave it away. Then her eyes trailed down. That grin oozed into a frown. She finally realized how clear the water was. Judging by the sweep of her eyes, she saw all the way to his toes. She now had come to understand that he could see all the way to hers, too, and everything above them.

Slowly, as if he might not notice, she covered her breasts with an arm. "Look, I'm going to swim back over and get my clothes on. Don't turn around until I say it's okay. Got it?"

"Yeah. I've got it." He coughed one more time. This time there was no alternative because he specifically promised, with no whispered contingencies, and a promise is darned near gospel to a ten-year-old, going on eleven.

By the time she sounded the okay, he turned to see her fully clothed and wringing water from her long strawberry blonde hair. She ran a few steps then stopped and turned back. "Remember what Momma told you. Be back up to the house by sunset." She then disappeared through the trees.

Ethan climbed up on the rock and sat, reflecting on the excitement of the past few minutes. He used his hands like squeegees pushing water from his chest and legs.

"That was a first for you, wasn't it?" came the voice.

"Yeah, it was," he said, no longer shocked by the suddenness of the voice. He looked around. "I can't see you."

"I'm working on it."

"What do you mean, you're 'working on it'. You're kiddin', right?"

"Sort of. Remember that age of innocence thing I explained to you?"

"Yeah. So?"

"Well, that's my problem. Not a big problem, I grant you. But it will be soon enough." The voice seemed to be moving in close behind him.

Ethan looked over his opposite shoulder and there he was.

"Your fascination with the female body caused me to work a wee bit harder, just so you could see me."

"For real?"

"For real."

Ethan tried to look serious. "I'm feeling bad about that. I shouldn't have peeked. I'm sorry for doing it."

"No you're not," the young man said then rolled his eyes and laughed. "In fact it was inevitable."

"What does 'inevit...unavit...vetable...whatever that word is; what does it mean?"

"It just means if it hadn't happened today, maybe it would have tomorrow, or if not this week, then maybe the next. When it happened was entirely your choice, but the desire to do it was programmed into you before you were born." He sat beside Ethan. "Besides, it's really not a question of whether you looked or not, but what you do with the information."

"What should I be doing with it?"

"Learn and know. That's all. For example, you now know beyond doubt you and your sister are different. It should make it easier to understand that she doesn't think quite like you do either."

Ethan remained quiet for a moment. "I guess you mean I don't need to apologize to her. Is that it?"

"Wrong. You should apologize, but not because you peeked. You should ask for forgiveness for abusing Jessie's trust." The young man flicked twigs as he spoke. "Soon your sister will need someone she can trust."

"You're startin' to sound preachy."

"Sorry, just feelin' a little time pressure to get the information out. I suppose that does make it sound that way."

"That's okay. Would you do me a favor?"

"What might that be?"

"Let me watch you disappear."

"I can't do that."

"But if you're a ghost, what difference does it make?"

"I never said I was a ghost. You said that. I'm your friend was all I ever told you. I just like dropping by and visiting with you." The young man walked behind the youngster, but this time Ethan made sure not to let him out of his sight. As the young man forced him to look back over his other shoulder, the late afternoon sun blinded Ethan but he still saw the young man's darkened silhouette.

"Your family has weathered one bad storm and, now, a storm of a different kind is coming." You'll have to help your father find reason out of turmoil."

Tears dotted his cheeks from the strong sunlight as he looked into the shadowy featureless face of the young man. Ethan fought to keep him in sight but succumbed to the strong glare and rubbed his eyes. When he again opened them, the silhouetted figure was gone.

"No, wait. I don't know what turmoil means. How can I help Daddy if I don't know what that is?"

A sudden gust swirled leaves from the surface of the rock where he sat blowing them toward the tree line. A voice rode in on those leaves. "When your family is at odds, angry and confused, ask your dad if Jessie is any different from other teenage girls."

"When will that be?" He became almost desperate looking for the young man to reappear.

"You'll know," came the fading reply.

Chapter Six

The young man's warning about some unknown kind of trouble in the family shadowed Ethan. He noted every detail of his family's life but, truth be told, he didn't know what he was looking for. It boiled down to and hinged on that one new word he'd learned, "turmoil".

June ended and July was halfway there. It was worrisome. As the days slipped from one to the next, he came to believe the event, whatever it happened to be, had passed with no consequence. He didn't know how much discontent constituted turmoil; there'd been arguments but nothing unresolved by day's end.

Standing next to his squatting father in the cotton field like an enlisted man beside his commanding officer, Ethan gazed across the seemingly endless rows of fragile just emerged seedlings with only two leaves per plant, the most vulnerable stage. This fretful ritual had become daily for his father as if all these tiny tender plants called to him like lost babes in the woods. His father remained close and checked them often. How that helped, Ethan couldn't say.

"It has a good start," he told Ethan, sitting on his heels gently fingering the leaves of a tiny plant, "but it's going to be a nail-biter right up 'til harvest..." He sighed. "...If it makes it at all."

The concern in those words Ethan also saw in his father's face. He wanted to say something encouraging but could think of nothing. Staying close in case he was needed was all he could do. Now that there was no turning back, it was entirely up to the season, the weather and the bugs. Compelled to contribute something to the conversation anyway, "I guarantee ya it'll be a great crop, Daddy."

"Guarantee, huh?" Sid looked up at him and offered a patronizing smile. "That's a mighty strong word. It doesn't leave any wiggle-room." He jostled his hair. "I'm inclined to take it though."

Ethan smiled and shrugged. He wanted to run down to the creek and chat with the stranger. He needed advice, but all recent attempts had failed. He suddenly straightened. *Maybe he's not comin' back, that age of innocence thing.* Suddenly flushed, he looked down the hill toward the creek.

Maybe I'll never see him again.

Sid sprang to his feet. "Oh well, there's certainly nothing I can do about the crop at this moment." He dusted his hands. I wonder if your momma has breakfast ready yet?"

Ethan hadn't realized he was hungry until his father mentioned it. He looked to the back door of the house, about fifty yards away up the gentle slope. "Come on, Daddy, "I'll race ya."

His dad made a quick move.

Ethan squealed and bolted sprinting across the cotton rows in his bare feet slowing only to avoid a patch of goathead thorns. He didn't dare look back. If he took the time, his father would overtake him for sure. Eyes straight ahead, he focused on the backdoor. He held his breath. His leg muscles burned. Still, he didn't look back. Lungs about to explode, he jumped up onto the back porch and let it all out in a single huff falling forward hands on knees unable to suck in enough air at first. He then spun to verify his margin of victory.

His father had not run a single step. He wasn't even walking, just watching the show, grinning. Sid pulled his green cap off and ran a confident swipe through his light brown hair then replaced it. "Whew! I'm tired. How about you," he shouted.

"Aw, Daddy." Ethan's hope for his first legitimate win had been dashed.

"Sid!" his mother called out from behind the screen door and over his head, "Hurry and get up here. We've got a problem with Jessie."

The comment confused Ethan. Jessie wasn't home, having spent the night with her best friend Mandy Hargrove, a planned sleepover she'd looked forward to for days.

Sid trotted to the back door.

"Mandy's mother, Emmy Lou, called a few minutes ago," she said. "She told me the girls apparently slipped out of the house some time during the night. She's worried sick. She's already called everyone she can think of and can't find them anywhere."

Sid doubled a fist and pounded his open palm with it. "Dang it! I'll ground her 'til her twenty-first birthday," he grumbled then slapped his thigh with his cap. "Let me wash my hands then we'll go look for her." On his way to the bathroom, the phone rang.

Ethan's confusion worsened. *Why would they sneak out of the house in the middle of the night? It's way too dark to have any fun.*

His mother answered but he only heard her side of the conversation. It sounded serious. "Where, sheriff?" She listened for a moment and repeated, "Where?"

A relieved look came over her. "So, you're going to bring her home?" She pinched the bridge of her nose.

Ethan tried to figure out what was said. He wanted to know what had happened too.

"Thank you, sheriff. We appreciate you allowing us to handle this situation within the family. We certainly promise appropriate disciplinary action." Her final comment still provided no clue, except that punishment would be involved, maybe even a whipping. His curiosity burned hotter. He stepped close to his mother when he saw his father returning from the bathroom, wanting to hear every word.

Sid came into the kitchen. "Who was that?"

"Ethan, go to your bedroom," she snapped.

"But, Momma--"

"Just go!"

Hurt and feeling as though he'd just been demoted to a lesser member of the family, he stormed to his room and slammed the door. He paced in a circle, pouting and curious. He then heard what sounded like an argument. He listened through the door. The words were angry but muffled. He couldn't understand any of it. Unable to corral inquisitiveness, he opened the door, stepped into the hallway and flattened against the wall sliding sideways toward the kitchen--just far enough to hear.

"If that girl thinks she can get away with being drunk in a car at the lake with boys all night, then, by God, she'd better think again!" his father said.

Oh man, I can't remember the last time Daddy was this mad. He began moving back in the direction of his bedroom, but desire to know overrode good sense. He stopped.

His mother, usually more demanding, seemed to be the calm one this time. "Now, Sid, we need to hear what Jessie has to say before we impose any stringent boundaries."

"Boundaries!" Sid exploded. "What the heck do you mean by 'boundaries'? There'll be nothing so voluntary sounding as that! Obviously the so-called boundaries she had didn't work."

That explosive rage called for yet another step toward his bedroom. Ethan became scared that simply standing within earshot might implicate him. It usually did. He could catch some of that anger and not even be the target. *Jessie's in deep chicken-doo now.* He couldn't imagine how things could be any worse for her.

Hearing the dull thud of car doors slamming, he raced into the bathroom to look out the window. Standing on his toes, he watched his momma and daddy walk out to meet a deputy. And there, head hung low, looking defeated, was Jessie leaning against the car. That long finely textured strawberry blonde hair was the only thing moving on her.

It seemed clear enough to Ethan that she didn't want to be noticed. But the way she was dressed ruined that chance. She had on low-rider jeans and a tank top cut high to expose her belly button and too much below it. If she didn't want to be noticed, that wasn't how to get it done. The anger on his father's face was clear as he grabbed Jessie's arm, almost yanking her off her feet and pulling her toward the house.

The muffled voice of scarcely controlled anger suddenly cleared as they came through the back door and after the screen door had slammed. "Get to your room right this instant and don't come out until I figure out what to do with you. I promise you, missy, it won't be pleasant!"

He couldn't hear if Jessie replied, but he certainly heard her wail as she ran by the bathroom on the way to her bedroom. The air seemed to thicken, as though two armies faced off. It became silent; a strained quiet that's absolute, waiting for the artillery and wondering who'd take the first shot. Anger and hurt so filled the air that it pressed Ethan into the bathroom wall.

Waiting what seemed a silent eternity, he finally concluded he'd take the chance and try to get down to the creek where it was peaceful. He opened the bathroom door a crack and peeked out. He couldn't hear his parents and stepped into the hallway but then stopped. His heart skipped and face flushed, so afraid of being caught not staying in his room as he was told to do. As he eased past Jessie's bedroom door, he heard a soft, muffled whimper. It sounded as though her face might be buried in a pillow. As often as they bickered, he still couldn't stand to hear her cry. He lifted his arm to knock on the door. Fist raised, he paused, thinking she might not want to talk. But he felt terrible for her and followed through rapping lightly. "Jess, it's me. Can I come in?"

The whimper continued unchanged. Since he didn't hear *no*, he took that as a *yes*. Tentatively, he opened the door and pushed his head into the room and looked. Sure enough, Jessie lay face down, two pillows covering her head, soaking the bedspread with tears. "Jess, I don't know everything about what happened…in fact, I don't know anything, but I wanted to tell you if you need me, I'm here."

The whimpering changed tempo. She appeared from beneath the pillows, gasping. "They don't trust me."

"Well, maybe not right now, but I'm sure they love you. I think you scared the bejesus out of 'em, that's all."

"I don't believe that. They don't trust me *and* they don't love me." The weight of her conviction drove her beneath the pillows again, sobbing.

Ethan sat on the bed next to her. He searched for words. Nothing came to him. And, then, he remembered the young man's admonition about trust.

"Jess, I really can't speak for Momma and Daddy but *I* trust *you* and I know for sure you can trust *me*."

Jessie sprang to a sitting position and hugged Ethan's neck. She cried. "I'm so sorry for treating you like I do. I should never talk to you the way I have been."

"Back off, would ya? I can't breathe."

She snapped her head back and let out a thready laugh. "Sorry." She swiped tears from her cheeks. "For a 10-year old twerp, you certainly seem to know the right things to say and the right time to say them."

"There's nothing I can do about any of this but I can listen."

Clearly, Jessie gave consideration to the wisdom of sharing information with her younger brother. But there was an answer in her expression; she had to tell someone; she had to let it out.

"We didn't do anything bad. All we did was split a six-pack of beer among the four of us, danced to the car radio and just enjoyed the night. I only let Bobby Arnell kiss me one time all night." Her face again tightened as fresh tears rolled. "Just once, for cryin' out loud! I can't believe I'm in this much trouble over a can of beer and a kiss."

"I don't think it has that much to do with beer or boys. I think it has to do with the trust thing. They didn't trust you to let you date, you didn't trust them to share your plan and, now, it's back to not trusting what you might have done last night. Somebody has to start trusting."

She looked suspiciously at him. "Have you been talking to Momma and Daddy?"

"Good grief no; I had to sneak in to the kitchen to hear what was going on because they ordered me out of the room."

"The way you said that sounded like something an adult would say."

"I did have a little help understanding the importance of trust, but not from them."

"Then from who?"

"Never mind. Just remember it. Geez, girl, what's it gonna take?"

She dropped her eyes. "Sorry. I do trust you, really. I've just never heard you sound so…so grown up."

44

"Really? Ya think so?"

"Yeah, twerp." She lightly slapped his nearly bald head. "You're making me feel like the little sister, not the older one."

He scooted off the bed and headed for the door. "I'm gonna see if I can find out what's goin' on."

"Don't get yourself in trouble."

Opening the door, he stepped lightly into the hallway. "I'm sure not tryin' to." He gently closed the door behind him.

Turning the corner into the kitchen, he saw his mother at the sink washing dishes, her back to him. It was one of those times that she appeared smaller than usual. Even the poof in her hair created by a loosening ponytail couldn't pump up her stature at the moment. Usually his mother was the strong-willed disciplinarian, but not right now. He heard her softly crying. "Are you okay, Momma?"

She flinched. "You startled me. Don't sneak up on me like that." She kept her back to him. "I'm okay, honey. Go outside and play."

As he left the house, he wondered if all this stuff was what the young man referred to as "a storm." If it wasn't, then he had no clue how much worse it had to be before it could be referred to as one. Looking around for his father, he saw Sid carrying two large buckets into the barn. Ethan recognized them as temporary storage for used nuts, bolts and washers. He figured his father was going to spend time sorting them and placing them into appropriate bins. He then heard the metallic clang and tinkle of metal hitting the concrete floor in the barn. Once he'd walked to the big sliding door covered in rust-pocked corrugated metal, he saw that's exactly what his father was doing. He didn't know why, but whenever his father needed to solve a problem, sorting nuts, bolts and washers seemed to help sort thoughts, too.

"You need some help, Daddy?"

"No," he snapped. "Go play."

Ethan didn't know if he should say anymore or not but then figured things hadn't cooled down enough yet. As he hesitatingly began to walk away, his father looked up.

"Ethan, wait a minute. Come on back. You can help if you like."

He approached slowly, as a hunter approaches a wounded lion. Without saying a word, the youngster turned over one of the buckets and sat on it then grabbed a handful of washers. He began piling them according to size.

He said nothing.

His father said nothing.

After a time, Ethan felt terribly uncomfortable and finally said the only benign thing he could think of. "It's sure a nice day today."

Sid looked at him. His father seemed to probe him with his eyes.

Ethan thought he saw the birth of a smile.

"Nice day, huh?" Sid's face started to change, turning more pleasant. "I guess I haven't noticed."

"Maybe a little too hot though," Ethan said as casually as he could.

His father then, indeed, smiled.

He wanted to ask about Jessie but remained nervous about tipping some scale holding his father's emotions in check. He began to speak, but at the last second, held it. *Is this the time the stranger was talking about?* His stomach twitched but then decided to go for it. "Daddy, he blurted, "What Jessie did; was it any different than what any other teenager might have done?"

He quickly pulled his eyes away from his father and dropped his head. He feigned more interest in the stack of washers in his hands than his father's answer, but glanced in jerks, watching for signs of anger. To his great surprise, all he saw was a total lack of expression. "I mean…I don't know, I just thought any teenage girl would do the same thing, you know, if they had the chance."

Still, his father sat stone-faced letting a bolt slide from his fingers and clank upon the floor. He dusted his hands.

Ethan became very afraid he'd just lit the fuse on an explosive and violent tantrum that seemed to be building and appeared imminent. "I'm sorry. It's none of my business." He broke eye contact and busied his hands.

"You're right on both counts," his father said. "It isn't any of your business and…" He paused, chewing on the inside of his cheek. "…she probably did no worse than any girl her age would have." His expression was distant, like his mind had latched on to a concept that pulled him somewhere far away from where they sat. "Maybe it's time to establish guidelines and let our little Jessie spread her newfound wings and see if she can fly alone."

His father's eyes cleared and Ethan became the focus. "Finish sorting these and put them in the right bins over there. I need to go to the house and have a heart-to-heart with your sister."

He scratched his head. *Did I just save my sister's butt by asking that question?* "Cool."

Then regret settled on him when he saw a formidable mound of nuts, bolts and washers. He'd gotten himself into a chore that'd take at least an hour to finish by himself. "Doggone it!"

Chapter Seven

Ethan floated on his back. Face barely above water and with the gentlest push of his hands he turned lazy circles watching puffy cumulus clouds drift by, assigning names or titles to each. One, beyond the overhanging cottonwood tree, with a wisp coming off the top, reminded him of his sister's hair on a windy day.

That reminded him of a less pleasant event two days ago that came barreling in to crash his cloud watching party. He couldn't get his mind back on the game. *I wonder what Daddy told her?* Curious as he was, it was unimportant that he know specifics. He took comfort in the lack of tension in the Lee house. *I don't think I could stand more turmoil. Tur...moil. Cool word.* He took in a mouthful of water and spewed it into a miniature geyser feeling good about the part he played.

"It does feel pretty darned good. Doesn't it?" the voice said.

Startled, Ethan gagged on the remaining drops of creek water still in his mouth. He splashed around and faced the direction the question came from. Appearing just as he did when he disappeared before, the young man stood silhouetted as a dark figure against the brilliant July sun. "How do you know what I'm feeling?"

"Just a lucky guess, but I've gotten pretty good at it, don't you think?" He folded his arms across his chest and, as a cloud crossed the sun, Ethan saw smug satisfaction on his face.

"Yeah. Right. Where have you been? I needed help and you were nowhere around. Nowhere, I tell ya. Some friend you're turning out to be." He cupped his hand and hit the water, fully intending to splash him.

The young man watched the incoming splash. It seemed to follow, then fall, where his eyes directed. The arc of the airborne stream took an unusually sudden downturn and fell at his feet. Ethan tried again. It looked as though the water refused to land on the young man.

"You didn't need me. You just thought you did."

"I darn sure did." He hoisted himself up on the lower surface and sat. "Dang, I got scared. The only thing you told me was that question I should ask Daddy and to work at gaining Jessie's trust, but you never told me when to do those things." Ethan tried to manufacture anger but annoyance was all he could muster. Then, even that went away. Even so, he brushed cottonwood twigs from beside him into the water and slapped the rock to show his displeasure.

"Do you remember when I told you that you'd know when the time was right?"

"Well, yeah. But--"

"And you did. Case closed." The young man bowed then applauded Ethan. "You turned problem-solving into an art form. It was magnificent. I'm proud to say I know you." He squeezed Ethan on the shoulder dropping to sit beside him.

The stranger's hand felt cool. Ethan could have sworn he whiffed a chilled blast of fresh air, like the smell right after the first snowfall. "Hey, are you that guy who gave me and Daddy a ride on that cold day last winter when our truck broke down on the highway just outside Plainfield?"

"Nope. That was someone else."

He snapped his fingers, "Doggone it," then waggled one of them at the stranger. "I still say I've seen you before. I'll remember soon, so, why don't you just go ahead and tell me your name now?"

"My name's not important, but things that need taken care of are. My time with you is limited. Besides, it'll come to you. I promise."

"Well, I think it's important." Ethan brooded then thought about the stranger's comment about limited time. "Okay, no more dodgin' the question, how do you know all the things you do?" He climbed to the higher rock shelf above them.

"Let me answer that by asking, why do you like sitting up there, at the highest point, rather than down here beside me?"

"That's easy, I can see up the creek to check out what's about to float by and, if I want to, I can watch it until it's out of sight the other way." He brimmed with confidence that he'd explained it with intellectual flair. "Your turn."

"Well let me just say that I like sitting up high too. That way I can see what's coming and I can see what's going...all at the same time. But what I'm seeing upstream is usually many different small tributaries that come together and become one larger flow of water as it passes. Once it passes, it remains a single body of water downstream forever. You and I, little man, are making sure the right tributaries come together to feed that one big stream. Now you know. Happy?"

"That doesn't explain how you know things?"

The young man laughed. "I just answered that."

"You did?"

Ethan tried to think about what the stranger had just said but could not seem to apply it to the question he'd asked. *What in heck has making a big stream from smaller streams have to do with knowing so many things about my family?* "You're givin' me a headache."

"Just don't forget what I told you. You'll come to understand it in time. Now, to the business at hand: Your momma and daddy are taking you to town Saturday to play miniature golf. Right?"

"Yeah, how did you..." Ethan held up his hands, "Never mind."

"Wouldn't you rather go see that new movie? It's still showing at the Regal in Plainfield. I hear it's a gem-dandy."

"I'd rather play miniature golf this week. All my friends will be there. Maybe I'll go see the movie next Saturday, if Momma and Daddy'll take me back to town."

"Would you change your mind if I said the movie won't be showing after this week?"

50

"Really?" Ethan suddenly wondered about the wisdom of his choice. "I guess I can play miniature golf anytime. I'll see most of those guys soon enough. Besides, the miniature golf course will still be there next week, right?"

The young man didn't attempt to answer, just waited for Ethan to bring his thought to conclusion.

"And, the movie will be gone." He paused and weighed his options.

"What do you think?" the young man asked.

"Okay. I guess you're right. I'll go to the movie Saturday."

"I promise that you'll look back and see it was a wise decision indeed."

It seemed far too unimportant to be considered wise. *Maybe I'd better look that word up.*

Looking down to the jutting rock below, "But why…" The young man wasn't there. Ethan looked across the creek, behind him, left, right--but he was gone. "Hey, where'd you go? Come on now, don't bail on me again." He looked from tree to tree trying to catch sight of the young stranger. He didn't see him anywhere. "Doggone it, man, it's not funny, you leaving me confused like this?"

"Who are you talking to?" came a different voice from across the creek.

The sound of his sister scared a knot in his stomach. "Uh, no one…just myself."

"Well, don't start answering yourself," she said then laughed. "I'm better prepared this time." She gingerly stepped into the water, splashing a little onto her upper thighs and stomach, easing into the bracing coolness. "I actually planned to go swimming before leaving the house this time." She wore a faded well-worn pair of snug denim cut-offs and a tight fitting red tanktop; good creek swimming clothes. She'd pulled her hair back and bound it in a tight ponytail.

"Dive in and come on over."

Jessie walked until it became too deep to stand then gently leaned in to the water and dog paddled over. She pulled herself up and sat below her little brother. "I really came down here to talk to you." She wrung water from her ponytail.

He pulled his head back, surprised. "Really? What about?" He couldn't imagine what his sister would have to say, unless it just happened to be an opportunity to take a few verbal jabs like she usually did.

"I have to know what you told Dad yesterday. He apologized for getting so angry. Then he and Mom told me I could start dating...provided I follow some tight rules." She shook her head in disbelief. "What the heck did you tell him?"

"Nothing, really," he said with a shrug. "I just asked if what you did was so different than what any other teenager might have done if they had the chance." Ethan still had trouble, too, believing he changed the outcome of such a delicate situation with a simple question. But, the undeniable proof sat on the rock below him in the form of gratitude from a most unlikely source. He saw softness in her he'd never noticed before, at least not while looking at him. *Jess is really sort of pretty...for a sister.*

She pressed her lips into a thin white line. "Well, twerp, it looks like I owe you a favor." She clearly wanted to maintain sisterly belligerence but couldn't. "Things you've said and done lately are getting a little spooky. What do you know that I don't?"

Putting on his most adult face, he purposely appeared to ponder the weighty question. "Do you know why I like sitting high on this rock?"

"What's that got to do with anything?"

"I like to sit here because I can plainly see what's floating by. Now, do you see where I'm going with this?"

"No."

"Shoot! I was hoping you did." He then looked away and muttered, "I don't have a clue either."

Chapter Eight

"Ethan, get your shoes on and get in the car or we'll leave you behind; ya hear me? His mother's patience had just run out. Frustration was an everyday occurrence for her. Still, he didn't want to be the focus of it on a Saturday morning. He wasn't as accomplished at letting it roll off like Jessie or his daddy.

He poked his head beyond his bedroom door and saw his mother tapping a foot with her arms crossed at the back door. "I'm tryin' Momma. Hang on." Hopping around on one foot, he wrestled a sneaker on and then the other. But shoes that were perfectly comfortable just weeks ago had now become oddly difficult to get on--too small and uncomfortable--toes jammed against the ends and pressed the sides. If it weren't his own feet causing the problem, he wouldn't have believed he needed a new pair so soon. Finally, he abandoned a finished look and ran down the hall, shoestrings flopping.

"We need to get to the miniature golf course before noon or you'll be standing in line between holes," his father said. "I don't think your buddies will appreciate it if you're the cause of it. Besides, I'm not sure I want to wait that long for y'all to finish."

Ethan stopped cold. It struck him that he hadn't told them his change of plan.

"Your momma and I don't have enough errands to keep us busy for more than a couple of hours. Believe me, hotshot, sitting in the car and waiting for you to finish is not in our plans."

"About that," he said, slowing to a walk, "I think I'd rather go to a movie instead...if that's okay with y'all, of course."

His mother stopped fumbling with an earring and faced him. "Seriously? All you could talk about earlier in the week was meeting Bubba, Aaron and Mikey at the miniature golf course. What happened?"

Fidgeting, he didn't want to lie but didn't want to divulge too much either. But he considered the possibility of a little fib to preserve his creek friend's anonymity. His mind was in overdrive attempting to frame an acceptable answer that might accomplish both goals. That's when it occurred to him he was woefully unprepared. All he could think to say was the truth: A strange man down at the creek just thought it'd be a better idea. But he couldn't say that. He began an answer even before he knew where he was going with it. "Well...I called Bubba and we wondered how long the movie would be in town. So, I called the Regal and a recorded message said that this was the last day. We agreed to save golf until next week...at least Bubba and I did. Aaron is still going to play miniature golf with some of the older kids. Then I called Mikey. He thought it was a good idea too. So, he said he'd meet Bubba and me there."

"Fine with me. I have to pick up the dry cleaning before they close at noon," she said. "Get those shoes tied and let's go. I'll be waiting with your daddy in the car."

Ethan breathed relief and rolled his eyes. *That was close.* Dropping to a knee, he took the time to put the final touch on perfect bows then jumped up and raced down the hall, past the kitchen, out the back screen door, letting it wham into a nearby rocking chair on the porch. As he leaped into the back seat his father said, "Hurry and shut the door, kiddo. Let's see what kind of adventure waits for us in town."

Melodramatically, his mother drew a deep breath and sighed loud and long. "Some adventure," she said. "Trips to the grocery store, dry cleaners and hardware store aren't what I'd call adventuresome." She turned and placed a finger on the end of his nose. "And you, little man, be sure and be waiting in front of the theatre no later than three o'clock. Got it?"

"Yes ma'am."

"That should be plenty of time to see the movie. I have to be home in time to start supper. Ya hear me?"

"Sure." He watched the countryside go by as his father monopolized the conversation the rest of the way in to town; going on and on about cotton, cattle and his hopes for high prices and a late frost. Ethan didn't mind. He preferred watching the scenery, scant as it might be. Telephone line poles kept his eyes springing from one to the other as they whizzed by. Cotton fields and the occasional farmhouse were about the only things to look at, but his eyes took it in and studied it all.

As they passed the Bower County Grain Elevator, Ethan suddenly became interested in the long line of kids already waiting to get into the miniature golf course only a couple hundred yards up the highway from the elevator. Speeding by, Ethan watched kids going in, putters in hand, laughing and shoving one another. A twinge of envy seized him. He puffed air into his lips, miffed that he'd agreed to go to a movie instead. Then he remembered making that promise he couldn't break. *Dadgummit!* He fell back against the seat and crossed his arms over his chest. *I just flat messed up.* He then quickly turned and pressed his nose against the back window, watching the small golf course as long as it remained visible. The gaiety of such brightly multi-colored architectural features was no help at all in confirming that he'd made the right choice. It finally disappeared from view, leaving him empty, as though he'd be missing out on great fun.

As planned, Bubba and Mikey waited by the ticket booth of the Regal Theatre. Sid stopped the car and held up traffic long enough for him to jump out. Waving goodbye, he joined his friends.

"It's not even hot outside today. We should've played miniature golf," Bubba said as his only greeting.

Mikey slapped Ethan's shoulder. "Yeah, we'll be about the only kids in the theatre." He then reluctantly stepped into the short line at the ticket booth.

Sour faces sapped his mood. He fell in behind Mikey. "Y'all might be right." He pulled his allowance from his pocket and carefully counted out the price of a ticket. "At least there'll be no line at the concession stand. That's gotta mean somethin'."

Tickets in hand, they entered the darkened lobby. He smiled trying to get their minds on a good time and off what they'd be missing but no good. They pouted. The usher took their tickets.

He felt terrible. "Just the three of us at the miniature golf park next Saturday…okay?" He cringed as he asked the question. A week seemed like a long, long time to a ten-year-old, going on eleven.

"Yeah. Next week," Mikey said with no enthusiasm, remaining down-faced.

Bubba nodded. "Sure."

The lackluster agreement did nothing to lift Ethan's mood. His spirit dropped to match theirs. And that was that--for a whole week. He sighed, bemoaning a decision that couldn't be changed.

Waiting a moment for his eyes to adjust to the dark, he scoped the auditorium and, just as they feared, no other kids their age were in the place. Watching the movie is only part of the movie-going experience.

Trailers of upcoming features lit the screen and flickered across their faces as they test-sat several different places before settling on a central location. Once the movie started and the fantasy began to unfold, it took the edge off his trampled spirit as he became involved in the plot.

Suddenly, a deep concussive blast rattled every loose architectural element of the old Regal Theatre building. Abrupt pressure on Ethan's eardrums scared him.

They ducked down.

Mikey slid off his seat into the floor.

Then the movie projector flickered and failed. It went dark and silent.

"What the heck was that?" Mikey asked.

"It could've been thunder," Bubba said.

Ethan shook his head. "I don't think so. I didn't see any clouds." The lights in the auditorium came back on. "It sounded like…a bomb."

Mikey's eyes widened. "Ya really think so?"

The three huddled closer, fearful that Plainfield was under attack by some dark, ruthless enemy.

Sirens began to wail in the distance, increasing in number, and seemed to be coming from different directions. Combined, they created a devilish music with no melody. "Whatever it was," Ethan said, hunkering down in his seat even farther, "it must have been really bad."

Bubba looked back to the double-door entrance to the auditorium. "I wonder if we can see what happened from the front door?"

Ethan's searching eyes stopped at Bubba. "I don't know. Wanna go see?"

Mikey was looking all around. "Everyone else has already gone to the lobby. Let's go see," he said, leaping to his feet and turning to run up the aisle.

The sparse crowd looked much larger jammed around the twin double doors, all staring in the same direction. Ethan scanned the gathering and began hopping about seeking a place to wriggle through so he could see what'd happened. An older woman holding the hand of a pre-schooler yielded as he pushed in beside her then on to the front of the group. Breaking into the open, he saw a lone cloud in a cloudless sky. But it didn't look like just any old cloud--odd shaped and out of place. *A thunderstorm? Couldn't be, wrong shape.* Then he noticed the cloud rose from a point that seemed to be much closer than he originally thought, maybe just the other side of town. "Is that smoke?" The question went up for grabs. He traced the outline of it with his eyes as it rose higher and higher into the sky. "What happened?"

"It might've been the Moorehead Cotton Warehouse," one said.

"I don't think so," another offered. "I see the roof of the warehouse. Whatever it is, is beyond that a ways."

An ambulance raced by on Main Street in front of the theatre, siren blaring. It sounded like emergency vehicles were traveling toward and converging on the mushroom shaped cloud from several directions.

"Whatever it is, it must have been really bad," someone said.

"Big, too," another said.

The group of people slowly pushed on through the two sets of double doors and moved out onto the sidewalk. The unspoken consensus seemed to be that whatever had happened was no danger to them.

An old pickup truck squealed to a stop on the street.

Someone in the crowd recognized the driver and yelled, "Hey George, what happened over there?"

"Bower County Grain Elevator exploded. A bulletin on the radio said fatalities are likely. That's all I know and all they're sayin' right now," the man said as a woman and young child climbed into the truck cab beside him. They sped away.

"What's a fatality?" Ethan asked the elderly lady behind him.

"It means people were killed, dear." She dropped her eyes and shook her head.

Hearing a car horn, Ethan turned to see his parents driving down Main from the opposite direction. His father squealed the tires to a hard stop then lowered his window. "Ethan, get in the car. Emergency vehicles and heavy equipment are moving in. They'll probably close the highway home if we don't hurry."

"Mr. Lee," the elderly woman asked, "Did you see what happened?"

"No, Mrs. Johnson, I didn't. But Faye and I were in the hardware store over a mile from the elevator and the blast blew out the plate glass display windows. There were a few people injured from flying glass who had the misfortune of being near the front of the store at the time. Faye and I were at the rear."

As Sid answered the lady's question, Faye waved with an impatient roll of the wrist for Ethan to hurry. He ran to the car, hollering over his shoulder to Mikey and Bubba, "I'll call y'all when I get home." He was too young to get his mind around what'd happened because nothing in life had ever happened to compare it to. He just knew it had to be bad because older and wiser people thought so. He slid into the back seat and wanted to quiz his father but the mood in the car wasn't right for questions. A morbid pall hung heavy in the air.

As they pulled away from the theatre, his father's face was a confusing mix of anger, sadness, and laser intense focus on the street ahead. "I'll take back

58

streets most of the way, but we'll still have to turn onto the highway near the elevator to get home," he said.

Why can't we go home the way we always do? Ethan wondered. *Why is Daddy going down all these streets I've never seen before?* The closer they came to ground zero, the true destructive impact became evident even to Ethan. Around a mile out, as his father had said, every building had windows blown out. Closer in, they saw structural damage--shingles gone, partial roofs, then a few walls blown down. By the time they came within a quarter mile, less substantial structures had been totally destroyed, collapsed and piled in rubble heaps. Fires burned sporadically.

Every emergency vehicle imaginable was scattered about, lights flashing in all directions. Firemen, policemen, sheriff's deputies, state troopers and helpful bystanders scurried about moving debris. Smoke billowed from numerous random locations. Ethan came to realize how people--a lot of people might be unaccounted for.

Sid crept along over-steering to avoid large chunks of concrete or wall sections that lay haphazardly in the street. Finally, they made it to the highway home.

Only then did the full impact of the young stranger's comments hit home. It resonated like a loud painful echo only he could hear. It came together like a train wreck in his head. A nauseating lump rose high in his throat as he looked to where the miniature golf park had been. He looked to the horizon ahead. Then he realized he couldn't even tell where it'd been. The sign, the ticket and concession building, the colorful course obstacles--everything was gone, as if swept clean. He questioned his judgment, looking up the highway then down. Then came to the only conclusion he could--it was gone.

"Oh, my God," his mother said, "The children…all the poor children." She cried.

Ethan scooted forward to the edge of his seat to see his father reaching across to hold his mother's hand.

Lifeless and injured people were everywhere. Ethan didn't want to look but couldn't stop; nightmarish snapshots burning indelibly into his memory. A saddened chill racked him. He cried, too.

With a jolt, his general sadness instantly became specific.
Breath left his lungs in a rush.

Aaron!

Bubba Watkins' older brother had chosen to play miniature golf.

Chapter Nine

Only a few hours after the grain elevator explosion, supper began quiet and, so far, remained that way. Ethan had no appetite, slumped over his plate absently dragging a fork through mashed potatoes taking only small bites for his mother's sake. Emerging from tragic thoughts, he glanced and saw his father's stare break off the instant Ethan's eyes met his. Then, looking around the table, he wished for the usual mealtime banter. He wondered if his momma and daddy, deep down, wanted to talk about it but refused to at the supper table. It was one of those subjects that if they did, he'd probably be sent to his room.

Finally, his parents began attempting conversation; the weather, grocery prices, laundry and other equally disinteresting things. He wanted to know what they thought about it; how it could've happened and why. But one thing was perfectly clear; they talked around it, not about it, jumping from one subject to the next, sentences short and chopped, neither looking up from their plates when they spoke. The only commonality was that the one topic on everyone's mind sat perched like a hairy monster in the center of the table and was treated as though it couldn't hurt anyone unless someone actually admitted seeing it.

Leave it to Jess to slip the knot on a sensitive subject. "Good thing Ethan and his buddies decided to go to a movie." The statement simmered as a question.

Ethan saw his mother make solid eye contact with his father, as if seeking permission to answer. Her shoulders twitched then she shuddered. "Oh, honey," she mumbled, "The very thought of what might have happened...I don't even want to talk about it."

That, apparently, was all Jessie needed to hear to press the issue. "Dad, what makes a grain elevator blow up anyway? There's nothing but wheat in it. Right?"

It appeared Sid's appetite was no better than Ethan's, as he drew trails in the gravy on his plate with the tip of his fork, occasionally shoving the meat around. "It's the grain dust, honey. Once airborne it becomes volatile if trapped suspended then exposed to a flame, high heat or even a spark."

Ethan listened with interest and, although he was too scared to do it, hoped she'd press on with the questions and she did.

"How come there aren't grain elevators exploding all the time then since grain and grain dust is what they all hold?"

The edge on his father's voice sharpened. "Best I can tell there're at least a couple of reasons. One, and most obvious, would be lack of adequate ventilation. If dust were exhausted out, as it should've been, then that would be one preventative measure. Also, I believe there are chemicals available to reduce or eliminate flammability of dust that can't be entirely vented to the outside."

"So..." Jessie said, "...it'd seem someone screwed up."

"Seems so," he said with a sigh. He dropped his head to continue the pretense of eating.

"There must be real idiots working there. Someone should be fired."

Angered by her flippancy, Sid dropped his fork in the plate with a loud clink. "I'm sure whomever that person turns out to be lost more than their dadgummed job if they were anywhere around that elevator today! People died today, Jess!"

His momma's eyes filled with tears. She excused herself and rushed to the bathroom.

Ethan began to understand the lack of conversation. Tragedy in which friends and neighbors were affected, maybe killed, could not be talked about calmly--not yet. The subject was still fresh and raw. But he didn't blame his sister. She hadn't been there and couldn't know how bad it was.

As his mother rushed from the room, his father realized too late that he'd spoken in haste. "I'm sorry, Jess. I shouldn't have snapped at you." He scooted away from the table and rose, unable to look her in the eye. Stepping to the back door, he snatched his cap from the rack but hesitated once his hand wrapped the doorknob. He looked back at Ethan with many unasked questions of his own.

Ethan offered a lazy smile, wondering if his father was thankful he hadn't played miniature golf or if something eerie and mystical might be going on. He got up to follow and took a few steps towards his father, wanting to explain why he'd made that decision but then stopped. *I can't. I promised.*

Ethan felt uncomfortable not knowing what was on his father's mind. But he deflated in relief when he saw that Sid seemed incapable of putting words to that look on his face. His daddy's increasing glances and questioning looks unnerved Ethan.

He'd been manipulated by a stranger into passing along information that averted family crises on two occasions, maybe three, if the late killing freeze thing turned out to be true in a few more months. Keeping the secret of his personal advisor had become difficult, more than he ever imagined when he made the promise. Then again, he couldn't say who his guide happened to be anyway. Keeping his existence a secret might be difficult, but keeping his identity unknown was easy.

Jessie was shocked to tears by her father's outburst. She clearly didn't expect such a verbal attack, even if he did apologize for it.

"Don't let it get ya down. Daddy's just feelin' sad right now, so is Momma."

His sister made no response other than throwing an arm up and sniffling, slipping back into her self-styled role of family target and victim. She rose, left the table and headed down the hall.

"Aw, come on, Jess. Don't worry about it." Head hung low, she disappeared into her bedroom.

Ethan suddenly found himself alone at the supper table with a head full of sad thoughts. But there'd be no talking to his parents or sister for a while. His only choice was to walk down to the place that always promised peace of mind and usually brought a smile. He needed it more than ever now, seeking to regain that carefree mood of only a few short hours ago.

Leaving the house, he walked into a blinding setting sun. No matter--he could walk to the creek blindfolded if he had to. Averting his eyes, he chose to watch a miniature world at his feet between the rows of cotton stalks, ignored on most days, but today it was the perfect distraction, a source of fascination. He wondered if that tiny world nearer the ground was any more at ease than the larger world around him. A horned toad had a beetle trapped on a low hanging cotton leaf. It seemed too large for the tiny reptile to eat, but its instinctive urge was to do just that and it kept it in the position of considering combat with the bug. The two creatures squared off in a motionless dual. Ethan fell on his belly to watch a bit of theatre on the ground. He wanted this miniscule drama to carry his mind to a different place allowing his imagination to take over as he lay in the warmth of the late afternoon sun, chin perched on the backs of his hands. The soft soil felt good, secure. The shade of cotton foliage provided relief from streaming sunbeams around the leaves. He watched the beetle and his would-be attacker but then noticed a loop-worm inching its way up the cotton stalk. He imagined it to be a huge tree in the darkest jungles of Africa hundreds of feet tall and the worm a mighty python slithering its way to a lofty place protected from things that might wish it harm. The heat of the setting sun moderated and no longer burned his skin. Instead, it felt comforting. *I'd like to be that snake, far above bad things that hurt people... so high nothing could ever touch me.*

Unaware how drowsy he'd become he dozed.

"Ethan?"

His eyes snapped open and he raised himself above the cotton stalks, looking toward the house to whoever might want him but didn't see anyone. He questioned whether he'd actually heard his name called or dreamed it. The bottom edge of the sun had sunk below the horizon. He now believed it must have been his imagination and resumed his journey--one he'd begun half an hour earlier.

Stripping his t-shirt off, Ethan slid into the water, swimming to the low jutting rock. He climbed onto it and immediately up to the overhanging diving rock. He sat, uninterested in swimming on this day fraught with sadness.

"That look of maturity is a nice look for you," the familiar voice said.

"I don't wanna talk to you," Ethan said.

"I know. Your dad is suspicious of your mysteriously well-timed wisdom."

He looked about and didn't see the stranger but, this time, didn't really care.

"May I sit beside you?"

"Whatever."

"It's a sad day. I know you're scared, wondering how many friends you might have lost. Your mom and dad are wondering the same thing. But this is a good time to tell you something. Will you listen?"

"I'm not goin' anywhere, if that's what you mean."

"You don't have to but I'd like for you to."

"Sorry. I didn't mean to sound mad." He looked left toward the source of the voice but still saw nothing. He then looked the other way just in case he may have misinterpreted the direction--nothing there either.

"Ethan, there's no such thing as an accident."

"You're crazy," Ethan said, tossing a pebble into the water with angry intensity. "That'd mean someone blew the elevator up on purpose."

"Not necessarily."

"You just love confusing me, don't you?" He noticed movement and glanced left. And there the young man sat. "'Bout time you showed up." He looked back to his dangling feet and wiggling toes.

"The word "accident" implies no human intervention caused it...and that's never so. It began with a bad decision followed by another and another. There could've been a smidgen of conscious inaction thrown in, a bad decision unto itself. Suddenly, a disastrous thing happens and it's labeled an accident. No one wanted it and no one expected it. But many conscious decisions came together to make it happen."

Ethan glimpsed the young man's probing eyes. "Why are you looking at me like that?"

65

"Just going slow, making sure you understand."

"I guess I do."

"Every one of those decisions had one thing in common; none were made with the well being of others in mind, only personal gain and selfish intent. It could've begun with an innocent decision to knock off work a few minutes early and delay a chore until the next day. Certainly not a big thing but even that small decision was self-indulgent. It's the downside of free will."

The young man again paused as he flicked twigs into the water then nudged Ethan's shoulder with his own. "Not a good thing. Right?"

"I suppose not." Ethan wrinkled his nose. "Is all this stuff you're tellin' me so I won't make bad decisions?"

"Of course. But that's a huge oversimplification."

"*Oversimp…*what?"

"I just meant it's only one little bitty piece of the puzzle."

"What does that mean?"

"As you get older, pieces will fall into place as life becomes clearer but no simpler."

Ethan flicked a dried chinaberry into the water. "How can I tell if a decision is bad or good before I make it?"

"You can't. That's human imperfection. But always think first how your actions will impact others. Every word you speak creates ripples, like that chinaberry you just flicked into the water. But, unlike that little wave that eventually disappears, your words and actions do not dissipate…*ever.* From the instant the words are spoken or the deed is done the affect is eternal, possibly magnified if future decisions are equally poor.

"I don't understand, but I have a feeling you already knew that."

"You will in time, Ethan. It's only important that you remember it."

"Ethan fell back on his elbows and eyed the stranger's profile. "Ever been to Denver, Colorado?"

"Nope."

"Oh. Just wondering, because you sort of look like one of the guys who worked at a mountain resort we stayed in last summer on vacation."

"I've got to go, but remember that things will return to normal. I promise." The young man effortlessly rose to his feet.

"I sorta knew that already." He looked up at the young man. "Gonna disappear now?"

"Nah, I'm just going to walk away."

"Really?" He watched the young man saunter off toward the big cottonwood tree that shaded the diving rock.

The stranger smiled over his shoulder. "Yeah, really. And, always choose your words carefully; don't forget that either." The young man walked behind the big tree as the leaves caught a gusty breeze and rustled near its top.

Had the stranger just walked away, or had he disappeared? The question overrode the more laid-back notion of just letting the guy go. He jumped to his feet and ran the short distance to the tree then entirely around it. But there was nothing to see. *I'm probably stupid for not being afraid of him.*

He didn't dwell on it, having weightier things to ponder.

Chapter Ten

Ethan counted days to remember the last one that didn't include a funeral or memorial service for a victim of the Bower County grain elevator explosion. It'd been twelve straight. Even then, that single day without one had been preceded by another string of them. He didn't try or want to remember that number.

Since that tragic day things had been a blur in the Lee house and now it was the first week of August. Wearing a stiffly starched shirt, strangled by a tie, covered over by a suit coat in the dog days of Texas heat was awful but he impressed even himself mastering a double Windsor knot in a tie that had become soiled by overuse.

He'd cried so much sadness no longer required tears as he grew numb to the drones of sermons and eulogies. Although now a hardened veteran, it didn't protect him at one, Aaron Watkins funeral. Aaron had been a friend, his best friend Bubba's older brother. Watching Bubba and his parents sitting in the front pew of the Plainfield Methodist Church clinging to one another and sobbing tore at his insides. He cried as if Aaron were a member of his own family.

"Give it time", the stranger had told him. *How long?* Ethan wondered. *Please, no more death.* Giving it time had to be the most difficult thing he'd ever encountered. Unfortunately, wait was all he could do. Whenever he became impatient, he thought about those who'd suffered a loss. For those people life would never be normal again.

The tragedy captured national attention. Stories and updates inundated television news networks. The folks of the Plainfield community were forced to relive it again and again--different pictures and words but the same old stuff.

The novelty of it became quickly lost as Ethan watched snippets of Aaron's funeral on television. The story spotlighted grieving and sobbing faces. He couldn't take reliving it and clicked off the television then went out the back door into the yard with no destination in mind. He wandered and thought.

Bubba had turned eleven two days after the explosion. There'd been no party or recognition of it because the Watkins family had been mired in grief. He'd be celebrating his own birthday Saturday and felt guilty about that. But within that blame, a brighter possibility suddenly came to him.

"Momma," he said, running through the door back into the kitchen, "I have an idea."

"You seem to have lots of ideas." She turned and looked at him with raised eyebrow and a pleasant smile. "Most of those notions you've come up with have been pretty good." She finished drying a bowl and put it in the cabinet above the sink then turned to fully face him. "Okay, Champ, what's your idea?"

"I was thinkin' that since my birthday is Saturday and Bubba's was a month ago…at a really, really bad time, would you and Daddy mind if we had a birthday party…you know, for both of us, here this weekend?"

His mother just stood there rocking her head side to side. But then slowly began to smile again. She pulled the cup towel from its perch on her shoulder with one hand while retrieving a wet plate from the sink. She wiped it dry and set it on the counter. "I think that's an excellent idea," she finally said. "Lord knows the Watkins need something to take their minds off the sadness."

Ethan hadn't thought of anyone other than Bubba until that moment, but he saw his mother's point of view right away. "Yeah, we can invite other kids and their parents too. The grownups can play cards or somethin' while the kids have a weenie roast and swim at the creek. How about that? Do you think Daddy'll mind?"

"I can't see why he would. I think it's a good plan and believe he'll think so too."

Pleased, he then marched away, hands stuffed deep in his pockets. *Boy, oh boy, oh boy.* He saw a ray of hope that all would be okay. It'd be a great time and only two days away.

Ethan couldn't sit down the remainder of the day, thinking and anticipating. Each time he went back into the house his mother was on the phone inviting neighbors over for a Saturday afternoon shindig. He saw her go way beyond simply agreeing to it; she ran with it. The only serious preparations were those phone calls and an extra trip to the grocery store.

Expectations running high, he wasn't drowsy come bedtime Friday night, certain he wouldn't be able to sleep at all. But sleep did come--quite suddenly.

He found himself standing on his favorite high rock overlooking the creek. He looked up and saw the stranger casually sitting in the tiptop of that huge cottonwood tree on a limb that shouldn't have been able to support a grown man, or even a crow for that matter. His arms were casually folded over his chest and his ankles were crossed as he playfully swung his feet to and fro totally balanced on a twig that should be breaking and dropping him to the ground. Ethan marveled at it.

The young stranger simply looked down and smiled. "Ethan, I need you to remember something." Although far off the ground up in that tree the sound of his voice seemed to be whispered directly into his ear.

"Okay."

"Control your anger even if it hurts."

"Whaddaya mean by that?"

The young man faded away, then the tree, then the creek.

"Wait! I don't understand."

He woke repeating, "I don't understand."

Still dark, it was shortly before dawn Saturday morning. He pulled the covers up below his chin. The dream was weird but startlingly clear. He lay awake staring into the dark thinking about it. As the image and question looped in his mind, he drifted back to sleep--dreamless this time.

Later, a narrow ray of sunshine pierced his eyelids shining through a gap in the curtain panels. *Oh, boy. It's Saturday!* Instantly awake, he leaped from bed and got dressed.

At the breakfast table, his mother and father set rules for a party at the creek. First, a lecture on fire safety from his father then his mother embarked on the importance of watching out for one another while swimming, no dangerous horseplay.

"Whether you boys use them or not," Sid said, "I insist inner tubes be floating in the water in case someone chokes and can't make it to shallow water alone."

Ethan fidgeted. Every caveat heaped additional responsibility on him because he knew that he and his buddies had always engaged in rough and tumble play. Good sense might be scarce.

"The fire for the weenie roast must be surrounded by rocks, a safe distance from trees and grass," his father said. "I think you're old enough to handle it without an adult watching over you." He slapped Ethan on the back.

The youngster took his father's show of confidence as a challenge, one that might open the door for more unsupervised privilege in the future. The rules were the price of fun without chaperones. He straightened, committed to justifying his father's trust. "You betcha, I'll get 'er done and done right."

Midday approached. Ethan speeded preparations, piling stones in a circle in the nearest grass-free area which happened to be just beyond the Chinaberry saplings that lined the creek in the weedless turn-row next to the cotton plants. As he collected firewood, he looked homeward and saw that a few of the neighbors had begun to arrive. From where he stood at the creek, he saw smoke coming off the propane grill in the backyard. His father cooked hamburgers.

He checked his own inventory of weenies, bread, mustard and relish. He looked into the ice chest his mother had brought down in the back of the pickup truck earlier. It was loaded with iced sodas. *Perfect.* Ethan's smile couldn't get any wider. *It's party time.*

Slamming the ice chest lid, he saw Bubba and Jeremy Slater walking down the turn row toward the creek. Jeremy, a year younger than he and Bubba was smaller with curly blonde hair and a smattering of freckles. Ethan watched Bubba laugh, shoving little Jeremy around. Jeremy didn't appear to be enjoying it. *What the heck are you doin', Bubba?*

As they came closer, he heard Bubba tell Jeremy, "You're just a little piss ant." Then he tripped the smaller boy, shoving his face in the dirt.

Jeremy jumped up, spitting and wiping dirt from his lips. "Stop it, Bubba!"

"Come on Bubba," Ethan shouted up the hill, "Don't be that way. Y'all come on down and get somethin' cold to drink. I'll build a fire so we can roast some weenies."

Turning his back on Bubba, Jeremy tried to put the episode behind him. Bubba didn't let it go, flicking the little guy's ear.

"Ouch!" he squealed. "Doggone it, Bubba! Stop it! Or I'll--"

"Or, you'll what?" Bubba sneered.

"Just don't."

Ethan looked toward the house, hoping to see others coming. A distraction that might take Bubba's mind off his cruel game, but so far, he and Jeremy were the only ones. "Soon as I get a fire started, we'll go swimmin' and work up an appetite," he blurted before Bubba had a chance to speak again.

Jeremy began to respond but didn't have a chance to get out a single word. Bubba shoved him in the creek with all his clothes on. "It looks like Jeremy wants to go right now." He laughed sadistically.

Although the water was only chest deep, Jeremy gagged, unable to regain his footing.

Ethan tossed him an inner tube. "Are you okay?"

Sputtering, "I think so."

Ethan whirled around, "Dadgummit, it Bubba! What's the matter with you?"

Bubba stopped laughing. "You wanna be next?" He began to stalk Ethan.

"No, I don't. Not yet and not like that."

Jeremy held on to the inner tube and watched.

"You seem pretty darned sure of that," Bubba said. He grabbed Ethan's t-shirt and tried pulling him toward the water.

Ethan planted both hands on Bubba's chest and shoved as hard as he could.

Bubba stumbled backwards and fell on his butt.

Angered, Bubba leaped up and charged Ethan.

This time Ethan just tried to hold him off.

Suddenly, out of nowhere, a double fist caught Ethan on the side of the face and sent him spinning to the ground. Holding his stinging cheek, Ethan's face reddened. He snarled, "You shouldn't've done that." His lip quivered. Tears of rage filled his eyes. He drew both hands into tight fists preparing to mix it up. His thoughts narrowed to getting revenge. He leaped to his feet and made a beeline for Bubba.

But then he stopped. With utter clarity, he remembered the early morning dream. The stranger had said, "Control it, even if it hurts." He put a hand on his cheek and felt the pain. Beyond that, he felt the heat of anger behind it. He closed his eyes and forced even breathing waiting for fury to subside. He relaxed. His fists opened.

"Come on Ethan! Gimme your best shot!" Bubba yelled.

Ethan's best friend was so mad and so ready, he slobbered.

"No," Ethan said, taking deep measured breaths. "I'm not going to do that."

"Then you're just a little piss ant too!" Bubba taunted.

"Maybe." He walked up to Bubba and placed his hands over Bubba's white-knuckled fists. "But, if I did hit you, it wouldn't make me feel good. Did it make you feel good to hit me?"

Bubba's angry eyes turned surprised. It must have occurred to him that hitting Ethan indeed didn't feel good, yet inexplicably was ready to do it again.

Ethan walked back to the ice chest and pulled two cans of soda from beneath the ice and popped their tops. Jeremy climbed up on the muddy bank. Ethan handed him one on his way to Bubba. Then he offered his best friend the other. "Jeremy," he said over his shoulder, "put your swimsuit on and enjoy yourself. Hang your clothes in that tree and let them dry out." He turned to Bubba. "Here. You drink this. You're bound to be thirsty. When you're finished, go swimmin'. While y'all are doin' that, I'll get a fire goin'."

It was obvious Bubba couldn't understand Ethan's calmness. It plainly was more powerful than a blow to the head. He dropped to the ground and cried.

Ethan now realized Bubba's grief surfaced as anger. He glanced at Bubba and knew by the reaction his buddy's short-lived career as a bully was over.

In a very adult show of appreciation, Jeremy Slater shook Ethan's hand and together, one on each side of Bubba, they helped him to his feet. Ethan noticed a group of kids walking toward the creek.

Ethan and Jeremy agreed that it should never be spoken of again.

Chapter Eleven

The passing of another birthday signaled the approach of autumn and the end of summer vacation. Ethan's birthday, the seventeenth of August, had always been the final reason for celebration each summer. *Two weeks 'til school starts, barely time to blink, sneeze and belch.*

The end of summertime freedom conflicted with the allure of becoming a fifth grader. But, the charm would only last until the first homework assignment, whereas the passing of summer would linger; that he was sure of. Still, curiosity kept him wondering just how different it'd be from the fourth grade.

As he rode into town with his father, a whirl of feelings spun out, topped by the bear that ate all other thoughts; next summer might as well be a lifetime away.

The usual pangs brought on by the end of summer were not as strong this year because it had been marred by tragedy--a huge black mark on an otherwise carefree three months. Love it or hate it, school would be the best way to remedy sadness that was slow to move on.

The whole community pitched in and assisted with the cleanup of Plainfield. He'd never seen such togetherness; the first time in his life to see neighbors as more than people just living in close proximity. Everyone became an extension of one another's family--diverse opinions, religions, races, cultures and lifestyles, but always ready to help.

Remnants of the grain elevator and all nearby buildings and other improvements had been bulldozed and carried away, leaving behind bare ground in a large swath. Passing the site where it had stood left Ethan tingling. Aside from the fact no crops grew in that space, the area had become indistinguishable from the cotton fields around it, flat and featureless. "Will they rebuild the elevator, Daddy?"

"Probably. But there's a mess of lawsuits to settle first. It might be a year or two before they do."

The site of the miniature golf park evoked other, more personal emotions. Sadness rose in his throat every time they drove by because it was accompanied by an image of Aaron Watkins with that silly mischievous grin, the class clown and practical joker. Although Aaron often picked on him, those times didn't matter at all anymore. All he remembered was the good stuff.

He looked away from the bare acreage where the elevator and miniature golf course had been. He worked his mind and heart away from it. If he couldn't set his mind on something else, tears might come. As they drove on toward the tractor dealership, Ethan thought on events of the previous weekend instead. "Daddy, how did I do at the party? Did I take care of things like you wanted me to?"

"You sure did. Your momma and I won't forget it either."

Ethan flashed his big white teeth tipped with brown water stains from Texas well water in a broad smile.

"You were very grownup about it and handled things just about like I would've." His father steered into an angle parking space in front of the John Deere dealership. "I'll only be in there a minute or so. How about just waiting in the truck?"

"Sure." He watched his father slam the pickup door and disappear into the store, having no desire to wander among rows of plow points, tractor parts and endless containers of lubricants--the whole place smelling of diesel from the repair shop in the rear.

"Very grownup acting," his father had said, and "handled things like he would have." *I wonder if this affects that age of innocence thing?* His eyes followed a flatbed truck with a super-clean green tractor on its way to a new owner. A tag wired to the steering wheel flopped in the wind. His eyes followed it but his thoughts were elsewhere. *I need to know more about that stuff.* As he watched sparrows fly in and out from under the sidewalk overhang in front of the store, it occurred to him the stranger at the creek made a point of saying that when he kissed a girl things would begin changing. He wasn't sure if that was merely an example or the catalyst. *If I kiss a girl, does that mean from then on I'll never see or hear him again?*

He watched his father put a shoulder into the door of the store, pushing it open, carrying a box loaded with things he'd need to service the tractor.

Ethan had many questions for his friend at the creek but never seemed to have a chance to get them all asked. The answers he got never seemed to clarify anything. *I've got to know. I sorta like havin' him around.*

Ethan appreciated every chance to ride into town, even if he didn't do anything but enjoy the trip. Even carefree summer days could become monotonous. He studied every store, house and car as his father drove by on their way out of town towards home.

Once there, his father handed him a hoe. "Okay, mister, time to cut the weeds out of the garden."

Farm chores were mostly mindless tasks, giving him too much time to think. But, it was the chore of the day and defined his afternoon. As he hacked away at uninvited plants among the rows of peas, onions and tomatoes, he glanced frequently toward the barn where his father worked on the tractor, getting it ship-shape for the remainder of the season. Ethan swatted gnats and sweat bees that gathered around his mouth, nose and ears and wondered if he might slip away unnoticed and enjoy the day instead of working, but then it'd remain undone and that fact couldn't be hidden. *Maybe if I flap my arms fast enough I can fly away. Or, I could just wait until Daddy turns his back then disappear like that stranger does.* Plotting an escape became the escape. Time passed faster than he expected. His task was done and it was only mid-afternoon.

Leaning his hoe against the front of the barn as his father had asked him to, he said, "Daddy, if it's okay I'm going down to the creek."

"Sure. Just be careful, ya hear?"

Ethan was already trotting down the hill, waving confirmation of his father's warning. Faye was hanging laundry on the clothesline and heard Sid's caution as Ethan trotted by her. She added her own. "Don't you pull any shenanigans that might get you in trouble down there," she said.

"I promise," he shouted back. His trot turned into a run. The lure of cool creek water strengthened as he did. Kicking off his sneakers, he pulled his belt a notch tighter on his blue jean cutoffs, preparing to dive in and feel blissful coolness on his sun-reddened skin. A sudden rustling of dry leaves brought him to a skidding halt. A startled raccoon jumped from a tree to the ground next to him and ran down the bank of the creek.

"Good grief! You scared the heck out of me," he hollered toward the swishing tail of the animal as it disappeared into the undergrowth. The shock gave him pause. He no longer wanted to hurry the experience, but rather savor it. He stepped into the water, moving deeper until it was up to his waist. He splashed it onto his stomach then his chest, moving farther out shivering anew with each step at each new depth. The rising water against his overheated skin was magnificent.

"Have you noticed each time you get in the water you can go a little farther out and still touch bottom?" the familiar voice asked.

Casually splashing water onto his chest, "I haven't really thought about it. But, yeah…I guess you're right." He looked around and saw no one. "I am eleven goin' on twelve now you know."

"That you are."

"I'm glad you're here. I have lots of questions," Ethan said.

"I know what you mean. I have lots of questions myself."

"*You* have questions? I sorta thought you had all the answers."

"For heaven's sake no. No one who's ever lived on earth has had all the answers," he said then quickly added, "Except for one, of course."

"Okay then, just answer one question," Ethan said.

"Just one?"

"Yeah." He looked around for the young man. He still couldn't see him anywhere. "Hey, are you going to join me or just keep talkin' to me from whichever tree you're hidin' behind?" He leaned into the water and dog-paddled to the low jutting rock.

"Well, that question was simple enough; yeah, I plan on joining you...eventually. Just give me a few more seconds."

Ethan pulled up onto the rock and sat. "Wait a minute. That's not the one question I wanted answered."

"Then why did you ask it?"

"Doggone it." He scanned the treeline. "Don't play with me like that." He looked the other way toward the big cottonwood and there he stood nonchalantly leaning against it with his arms hanging, fingers laced to the front, as if he'd been standing there all along. Ethan pointed an accusing finger at him. "Don't forget that you're trespassin'. I could tell my daddy to run you off and I'm sure he would."

The young man's smile never wavered, continuing to appear as if he were pleased with himself. "You're right. He probably would, but I have a feeling it wouldn't be because I'm trespassing." The young man sauntered over and sat beside him. "I apologize for taking your question so lightly. But, you have to admit that you left yourself open for that one."

"You think you're funny, don'tcha? Never mind, don't answer that. What I really want to know is how much longer you're gonna be comin' 'round?"

"It depends on you, not me."

"That age of innocence thing?"

"You got it."

"So, someday you'll just disappear and never come around again?"

"Ethan, I'll never be far way. I'll always be as near as your dreams and thoughts."

"But dreams and thoughts can be make-believe. I know you're real because I can talk to you. I kind of like having you around." He looked up to check out a cawing crow landing in a tree down the creek. A thought struck him. He snapped his fingers. "Hey, didn't you graduate from Plainfield High School?"

"Sure did."

"Then that's where I've seen you." He slapped his drenched cutoffs. "Hot dog, I've finally figured it out. I've seen you on the school campus at one time or another."

"Nope, you never have."

"Huh?" Ethan pursed his lips, frowned and snorted. "I'll figure it out." He waggled a finger. "You just wait."

"I know you will."

"You wanna swim down with me and see if that ol' catfish is still there?"

"No thanks. But you go ahead if you want to."

Ethan slid off into the water. "If I do, will you still be here when I come up?"

You know, for a kid that only had one question, you sure are asking a bunch of 'em." He laughed.

"I hope that's a yes." He sucked in a lung full of air and dove down searching the fissure until he saw the catfish suspended in the darkened recess. Ethan reached in and stroked its snout repeatedly with the tip of a finger. It didn't recoil as it usually did.

Eager to tell his friend about it, he looked to the surface and saw the young man. What he saw, or thought he saw, was strange. *He's not standing on the rock. It looks like he's floating in the air.* He tried making out the image through the distortion of rippling water but couldn't do it. He looked to the young man's feet. They didn't appear to even touch the rock. The glare from the sun added obscurity as it beamed at a hard angle across the young man's body. Curiosity aside, Ethan suddenly discovered he was short on oxygen and could wait no longer, kicking off hard to the surface. Breaking through to fresh air, he took a deep loud breath. "Ya know what?" he said. "For a minute, I thought you could fly."

"I get that a lot."

"I'm serious. From down there you looked like you were floating over the water but the sun was so bright..." Suddenly Ethan became confused. He looked in the direction where he'd seen the light streaming from. Only then did he realize the sun wasn't in that direction. Instead, it was on the opposite side and partially obscured by clouds.

The young man rose to his feet. "Go on," he said, 'but the sun was so bright'…what?"

Hesitatingly, "Forget it. I'm not sure what I saw."

"That's okay. Sometimes, people or situations appear one way, but if we take the time to look again, it may be different than our first impression. Yep, sometimes our eyes see what *is*, but that's only the end result of the *why*." Standing on the lower rock just above the water, he backed into the bottom edge of the diving rock and leaned against it, casually propping a foot on an uneven surface.

Ethan pulled himself up out of the water onto the lower rock and sat. "You mean if I see a nasty old man pickin' his nose, he may not actually be pickin' his nose?"

The young man laughed. "At this rate I'll be dropping by to see you for a long time to come."

"What do you mean by that?"

"Never mind." He stepped over and sat beside Ethan.

"I'm serious," Ethan said.

"I know you are." The young stranger leaned his shoulder into him and shoved playfully. "If you see a man pick his nose, he's *really* picking his nose. And, I'm sure it'd look disgusting."

Ethan nodded. "Yeah, it would."

"But what if just before you saw him with a finger in his nose, you found out that his nose was bleeding and that he was only reacting to it, trying to stop it; would that make a difference in what you thought about it?"

"Well…sure."

"There ya go. Sometimes, it's not what you see but what you know about what you see."

"Oh, I see."

"I knew you would. Can you remember it?"

"Why would I need to?"

"Sooner or later knowing that things aren't always as they appear will come in very handy. I wager it'll be sooner."

The late afternoon sun appeared from behind a passing cloud, burning Ethan's bare back. "Okay, sure," he said, again sliding off into the water then twirling around to see the leaves of the cottonwood react to a sudden wind gust. "But, I still don't see…" Ethan looked to every tree and bush. "Hey, where'd you go?"

No answer.

He slapped the water. "Doggone it."

"We'll talk again," came a whispery voice.

But Ethan couldn't be sure if it was a voice at all. It may have just been the rustle of leaves in the wind.

Chapter Twelve

Anticipation muddled his head. He lay on his back in bed the night before early school registration, very sleepy but still awake. Fingers laced under his head, summer events rolled through his mind like a loosely plotted movie-- some related, some not.

Since the last visit with his friend at the creek, he'd begun to write down questions, wanting to be prepared and undistracted by the stranger's smooth conversational style. He always came away with vital but vague information and bewildered. No matter how Ethan tried, the stranger always diverted his attention away from answers he wanted. He wasn't ready for the visits to end but feared they soon might, going the way of summer vacation. Twice since their last visit Ethan had marched down to the creek pad in hand prepared to quiz the young man. He didn't show up either time. The young man's last comment dogged him; "Things aren't always as they appear." Although it'd been asked as a favor that he remember, it sounded more like a warning.

The sight of lightning bugs set against the stars of a moonless sky through his bedroom window captured his gaze from under heavy eyelids. It was a cooler night than it'd been and the window was up. The song of the cicada lulled him. *I wonder if I'm going to see that old nose-picker we talked about?* His mouth took an amused curl as he drifted off to sleep.

~ * ~

Nothing exemplified the end of August better than a stream of cars, kids and parents pulling into the inadequate parking area of the Plainfield Elementary School on registration day. Ethan sighed, psyching up for the inevitable beginning of another school year.

"It's going to be like a zoo with no cages," his momma said with a cynical grin. She eased through the graveled auxiliary parking area across the road from the school searching for an open slot.

Ethan smiled at his mother's humor but it wasn't sincere. The prospect of confining school days yanked the vitality right out of him. "Yeah, let's hurry and get this over with."

It was a tight fit but she found a parking space and worked into it. "I certainly won't be doing anything to slow the process, kiddo." She killed the engine and began gathering papers from the seat next to her.

As they exited the car, he saw a very expensive looking sport utility vehicle pull into a space opposite theirs. He became interested. The vehicle and the people were unfamiliar. In a town the size of Plainfield new faces are big news. He watched a young girl get out, appearing to be about his age and she didn't look happy at all. He noticed, too, a couple of younger kids exit the back seat, a boy and another girl. Both seemed to be the same age, about six--twins maybe.

Faye slowly reached back into the car to get her purse then feigned doing a little straightening of her makeup in the outside rearview mirror. "Ethan," she whispered, "I think I'll introduce myself to that woman. It looks like you may have a new classmate."

Before Ethan could say anything, or his mother even said hi, the attractive young mother jumped from the vehicle, her face distorted and red. "Rebecca! You get over here right now young lady!" the woman yelled to the young girl's back as the youngster walked away in a huff.

The girl finally stopped but refused to face her mother, standing stiff and straight. Then, in a show of obvious defiance, she clenched her fists, crossed her arms and pulled her chin down onto her chest.

Her mother lost her temper, took a giant step forward and slapped the girl hard across the ear. "You'll not disrespect me that way!" she yelled then raised an open palm to do it again. "Do you hear me?"

The youngster collapsed to her knees and pulled her head deep into her shoulders, sobbing. "Stop! Please, don't hit me again."

But her mother did hit her again, clearly unsatisfied with a single slap on the head.

The girl fell over and covered her head with her hands and her mother slapped the backs of them a last time before returning to her vehicle to get the twins.

Faye smacked her lips in disgust. "That was totally unnecessary," she muttered.

Ethan looked around. He saw that he and his mother weren't the only people watching. The lady's over-the-top discipline captured the incredulous stares of a number of parents and children, all walking toward the elementary school building. The lady didn't seem to notice or care that every eye was on her. Parents he knew well paused to watch then reluctantly walked on whispering to one another, all converging in a huddle near the front double doors of the two-story red brick building.

The gossip buzz began. "Did you see how that woman beat that child?" one said. "I can't believe a parent could treat her *own* child like that," another lady hissed, turning her nose up and away.

As the parents added the mortar of disgust and the stones of indignation to their fortress under construction that'd be set firmly upon moral high ground, Ethan looked around for the young girl and caught sight of her walking behind her mother and the twins--head hung low, eyes red, cheeks flushed and lip still quivering. The girl's spirit had been literally slapped from her. With the hand of a twin in each of hers the lady walked briskly. The young girl followed as they breezed past the huddled group of parents. All eyes remained on the strange new lady and her children. No one said a thing as she passed, but only until she and the kids disappeared through the doors.

"Who is that woman?" Ethan heard someone ask. No one answered right away. Finally another said, "I've never seen them before. They must be new in town."

"New or not," Faye said with a resentful hiss, "We don't need people with that kind of anger around here. She'd better get a handle on that temper. Lord only knows what might happen to that poor child in the privacy of their home if her mother is that willing to become violent in public."

Ethan made a move for the door. "Momma, I'm gonna find Bubba and the rest of the guys."

"Okay, honey," she said in a syrupy way.

Ethan frowned. He didn't like it when she put on such a phony show of affection. All he remembered was how she yelled at him when she got angry. Then he thought about it. *Oh well, she did just slam that woman for being mean to her daughter in front of her friends.*

He followed the girl through the door and stepped lively to catch up but remained slightly behind. He walked in fast choppy steps to maintain a respectful yet friendly distance. "Hi," he said. He fell behind and again had to pick up his pace to keep up.

She refused to look at him but mumbled, "Hi."

"Your name's Rebecca, right?"

"Yeah," she said surprised. "How'd ya know?"

"I heard your mother holler it."

That embarrassed her. "Oh." She watched her toes as she walked. "I'm sorry."

"No, it's okay, really. What's your last name?"

"Sanders."

Wanting to cheer her up, he said, "My name's Ethan...Ethan Lee. I'll be in the fifth grade. How about you?"

"Me too."

Her mother looked back and snapped, "Keep up and don't dawdle, Rebecca. Let's get this chore over with."

She looked over her shoulder and connected with him for the first time. "Ethan, right?"

"Huh?"

"Your name?"

"Oh, yeah."

She offered a fast nervous smile then trotted to catch up with her mother and two younger siblings before the woman found cause to speak again.

He saw a group of his friends and Bubba split off from them and caught up to him.

But Ethan was more interested in watching Rebecca walk away.

"What's with the new girl? You like her?" Bubba asked.

He shrugged. "Dunno. Maybe."

"All the parents have already made up their minds about the mother. And it sure didn't sound good." He blew a breathy whistle. "Man, oh man."

"I know," was all Ethan could think to say.

Students scheduled for the fifth grade gathered with their parents in the classroom designated as homeroom. Following the wishes of the teacher, prospective students stayed at the side of their parents to expedite enrollment. Ethan and his mother sat in desks at the rear of the room. Two up and two rows over sat Rebecca and her mother.

Ethan couldn't understand why the twins were allowed to wander unattended throughout the room yet she had been so hard on Rebecca. He watched Rebecca's mother stare out the window, oblivious to the discourteous and disruptive noise the smaller children made. *That's not fair. She's letting those yard apes run loose.*

He then noticed the scowl on his mother's face directed toward the new mother. That's when he became aware others were just as perturbed. All strained to hear above the undisciplined squeals and laughter of the two youngsters. As the teacher spoke about the school year and planned curriculum, his voice necessarily clicked into a higher range to be heard.

Make them sit down and shut up.

The twins did as they pleased, playing in the back of the classroom. He turned his attention to Rebecca. Her gaze began to dart side to side as she became aware of staring eyes. She flushed with embarrassment and hid her face, taking comfort in the darkened well within her stacked arms. He couldn't be sure but sensed she might be crying.

After the paperwork had been done and everything signed, they were dismissed. It was official; another school year had begun. Ethan tried to keep sight of Rebecca. People poured from the room and he glimpsed her jumping into the middle of the streaming crowd as they slowed to get through the classroom door. He saw she didn't want to hang around and pushed her way through.

He hurried to keep up.

She forced her way out the classroom door, running down the hall through the open front double doors. He wanted to say something to cheer her up but didn't pursue it when he saw her sprint directly to their SUV. Taking time to chat was plainly not something she wanted to do. *Why is this bothering me so much?* He watched her get into the vehicle and slam the door. *It's her problem not mine.*

When Bubba and the other guys caught up to him, Ethan's mind was forced away from the situation and gave it no more consideration. By the time registration was taken care of and all the visiting done, it was lunchtime.

"How about we treat ourselves to a hamburger at the Dixie King Drive-In?" he asked his mother.

"Sounds good to me."

Faye drove them across Plainfield to the Dixie King. After they'd ordered, his sister and two friends wheeled in to the drive-in a few cars down. Jessie jumped out of that car and came over. "Momma, there's a lot of talk around town that a strange woman brought her kids in to register at the elementary school. Is it true? Did you see them?"

"I don't know if she's strange or not, but she certainly displayed an unusual amount of anger. It did appear strange."

Ethan had just taken a huge half-moon bite from his hamburger, not really interested in his mother's or sister's opinions of the day's events but the familiarity of his mother's words, "'appear strange", caused him to stop chewing. *Where have I heard that before?*

"Yeah," his sister said, "I heard one of the parents at the high school say the woman appeared a little loony."

There it is again. The woman 'appeared' a little loony. He swallowed the big bite of hamburger and took another. He tried to remember why "appear" sounded alarm bells in his head. As he thought on it, he casually watched the breeze blow through a cottonwood tree in someone's backyard across the alley from the drive-in.

Then he remembered. The young stranger had said, "Things aren't always as they appear". Could this be what he was talking about? Is it possible what everyone saw wasn't the whole story?

"Be sure the girls bring you home pretty soon," his mother told Jessie.

As he watched his sister walk away, "Momma, what do you think it was that made that woman act the way she did?"

"I don't know," she said, as if she hadn't given it thought.

"Is it possible she was already angry about something and, maybe, Rebecca said the wrong thing at the wrong time? It could be that the woman is pretty nice and, who knows, maybe that's the first time she ever hit Rebecca and we just happened to see it."

Faye stared and tilted her head. Then haltingly, "That's a pretty grown-up assessment you're making."

"Well? Could it be possible?"

Cornered by her own negative opinion, she was now forced to offer an answer. Still with hesitance, "It is possible...I guess." She stared through the windshield off into the distance. "The lady may be suffering from depression, a bi-polar disorder...or some other crisis in her life I suppose."

"Maybe we need to find out more about her first...I mean, you know, before we talk about her."

His mother had hundreds of questions on her face but none she seemed to be able to verbalize.

Ethan hoped she wouldn't quiz him. So, as he watched her lips try to form questions, he nonchalantly said, "I've heard that sometimes things aren't always as they appear."

He shoved the last bite of hamburger into his mouth.

Chapter Thirteen

Faye stood over Sid as he knelt in a cotton row thumbing an immature boll down the hill behind the house. "The woman just hauled off and slapped the thunder out of that poor child and then kept on hitting her. I swear she could've broken that youngster's eardrum."

Ethan emulated his father, sitting on his heels. The elder Lee's lack of expression seemed to indicate he hadn't heard a word his mother said, plucking a tiny cotton boll, rolling it between his fingers and then flicking it away. "It sure has to grow faster'n this," he muttered.

He rose, dusting his hands on his jeans. "So, there's a new woman in town with three kids and a temper, huh?"

Ethan came up at the same speed and time as his father. He dusted his hands too.

"Yep, that woman was sure enough angry all right."

He belched long and loud.

"Ethan Lee!" His momma pointed a stern finger at him. "Cover your mouth for goodness sake and say excuse me."

"Scuze me." He faced his father. "Man oh man, that hamburger at the Dixie King was great. Food just doesn't get any better'n that." Seeing his mother's less than enthusiastic expression, "But you're a great cook too, Momma."

She continued glaring at him but apparently had no intention of pursuing his lack of manners further. "We don't know why she was so angry." Still staring at Ethan, her face softened. "I'm ashamed to say I was quick to jump to a negative conclusion about the lady."

"What's her name?" Sid asked.

Faye let her head drop. "Well, you've just given me one more reason for shame. I didn't even introduce myself."

"Their last name is Sanders. The oldest girl's name is Rebecca," Ethan said. "She'll be in my class this year."

Sid pulled his cap off, scratched his temple and stared at one of the few puffy cumulus clouds floating by. "Sanders, Sanders. Humph. Name sounds familiar. I've heard it somewhere." He put his cap back on.

Faye snapped her fingers. "I know what I'll do. I'll call Principal Hadley's secretary, Mary Winn, get the woman's name and address and pay them a visit. I'll bake them a cake."

"I didn't think the school was allowed to give out personal information."

"They're not," she said with a devious glint. "But I've known Mary for years; she'll do it for me."

Once his momma's mind was set, a tiny ethical snafu wouldn't stop her from putting things right. She now had a mission to know the woman and her family better. The set of her jaw told the story.

After supper Faye called Mary Winn. Concealed within a friendly conversation about kids, the new school year and recipes, Ethan's mother casually mentioned the new lady and got the name easy enough, Pamela Sanders. She'd recently moved to Plainfield from Kansas City. Faye mentioned that it'd be neighborly to drop by with a welcome-to-the-community gift. Smoothly, she requested Mrs. Sanders' home address.

Missus Winn obviously balked.

"Do you even know her address, Mary?"

Ethan watched his mother masterfully perform a verbal dance.

"Oh for heaven's sake, what do you think I'm going to do...set fire to a sack of cow manure, ring the bell and run?"

Ethan snickered.

She frowned at him and waved him away.

Thoroughly amused and a smidgen proud, he watched his mother manipulate her friend.

"How about I bake two cakes and bring you one of them and take the other to Missus Sanders?" She paused, waiting for an answer.

Then, the woman he was proud to call Momma, added the crème de la crème of deal clinchers, "I'll bake your favorite."

Then she went silent. The offer hung in the air. A smile slowly came up on her face. She snatched up a pencil and scribbled on the back of an old envelope. An extra German Chocolate cake won the moment.

Satisfied with the way things were coming together, Ethan marched out of the house and sought other dragon's to slay and mountains to climb. He walked to the end of one of the cotton rows and just stood for a moment.

A fat old hen crowded his feet. "Follow me and I'll throw you in the creek." He stared at the bird. *I wonder if chickens can swim.* "Keep followin' me and we'll find out the answer to that question. I bet you can do a mean motorboat with those wings. If you can't, I bet you try extra hard to fly." What began as a joke ended as an honest quest to know if chickens could swim. Now he wondered if the old hen would actually follow him all the way to the creek with a little enticement. He couldn't remember any of the flock ever following him that far, usually losing interest along the way. Walking slowly and checking back often, the old hen followed.

After a hundred, or so, yards the bird tired of playing follow the leader and began scratching the soft plowed ground to find something on her own. Ethan pulled a big green horned tobacco worm from one of the cotton plants and walked back to her. It worked. The hen followed obediently all the way to the creek.

He snickered at the prospect of throwing her in the water. The answer to the riddle was at hand; would the bird swim or fly? But the old bird wasn't quite as stupid as Ethan believed she might be, stopping at the treeline, flapping up a cloud of dust and running squawking toward the house. "What the heck's the matter with you?" he yelled.

"Sorry. I probably scared her," the voice said.

He flinched. "I wish you'd stop doing that. You scared me." He scanned the trees bordering both sides of the creek. "Besides, I didn't expect you to be here today. Where are you?"

"I'm still coming. Be patient."

"If you're not here yet, how come you sound like you're standing in front of me?"

"A ventriloquist has nothing on me."

"A *ventrila*...what?"

"Never mind."

"Hey, where were you the last two times I was here? I called for you."

"I was close but I also knew you didn't really need me. You just wanted to chat."

"Well, yeah. Isn't that what we always do?"

"I guess it is. You're a smart kid."

"Something wrong with chatting all of a sudden?"

"Heavens no, chatting is how we connect and grow intellectually. How about we chat now?"

"I didn't bring my list of questions. I can't remember what all I'd written down."

"How about I say something while you try to remember?"

"Sure."

"First, you're timing was great at helping your mother look past her prejudice."

Ethan didn't understand but it sounded like a compliment. "Thanks...I guess."

"You're welcome...I guess. "Now, here's something else you need to know: Anger passed along is like handing someone a wildcat in a sack."

Ethan dropped heavily onto a tree stump and rolled his eyes. "Here we go again. You're tellin' me things I don't understand. Doggone it, man, why do you do that to me?" He reached to the bush beside him and let a ladybug crawl onto his finger. When he looked up, the young man was sitting Indian-style on the ground next to him. "Hey, I didn't hear you sit down."

"I'm a wee bit sneaky that way." He flicked a twig at Ethan's finger where the ladybug crawled. It flew off. "Now, about that confusion thing; let's say, for example, you're so darned mad you think you're about to explode…"

"I've sure been that mad," Ethan said with a tiny puff of arrogance.

"We all have. Let's call your anger the cat."

"Huh?"

"The wildcat and your anger…the same thing. Got it?"

"Oh. Okay."

"Then, you get tired of holding that sack, you know, keeping all that anger inside, so you hand it off to someone who loves and trusts you. While you're doing that, the angry feline leaps out and attacks that person…someone you equally trust and love. Now, here's the sad part of the story; the person on the receiving end is perplexed that you'd hand them something so hurtful. Understand?"

"Perplexed?"

"That just means confused."

"Oh, like me right now. You're one weird dude, ya know that? Do you really think I'd get pissed off and hand someone a mad animal in a bag."

"Boy, if your mother heard you talk like that she'd have a conniption fit."

"Well, stop telling me stories I don't know what they mean."

A wind gust interrupted the utter calm of the late August day, rustling the canopy of leaves overhead. The young man smiled and patted Ethan's knee. "Just because someone seems mad at you doesn't necessarily mean it's so. They may have unwittingly let the cat out of the bag. That's all."

"Now, what the heck does that mean?" He vigorously rubbed his face as if a pesky spider web had settled on it. He snapped his head back around to try for clarification but the young man was gone. He sprang up, marching up and down the creek bank. "Come on, don't leave yet. I don't have any idea what you're talkin' about." He continued pleading for a longer chat but finally gave up, dropping back onto his makeshift stool, the tree stump.

"Dadgummit!" He fell over, elbows on knees, and let his chin rest in his palms. "A sack full of snakes would be a whole lot more interesting than a

94

doggoned old wildcat." He sat bolt upright. "That's it! You're the fella that manages the produce section at the grocery store." He slammed a positive fist into his palm.

As the cottonwood bowed to a particularly hard wind gust, he heard a rustling whisper that seemed to follow the wind down the creek. "Sorry. Keep trying."

As it died away, all he heard were insects buzzing about his head and the ringing in his ears, two sounds consistently part of hot Texas afternoons in late August.

Chapter Fourteen

The days remained hot and the nights warm. September was shaping into an unseasonably warm month in what seemed to be an atypical year in the making. Weather reports showed all cold fronts that could have been season changers remaining well north and sweeping eastward across the Great Lakes and upper Midwest, leaving Texas to bake in summer like temperatures.

The first full week of school turned into an unremarkable collage of events, doing more to define the remainder of the year than provide a learning experience. So eager to be someplace else, Ethan caught himself holding his breath in class and consciously had to force resumption of breathing. Teachers gave talks on behavior, dress codes, homework, grades and on and on and on, everything about class work--just no class work. He viewed his opinion as an observation of events not a complaint. Although monotonous now, he didn't look forward to teachers droning on about obscure places or math problems that'd give him a headache for sure. In its way a blessing, because the current brand of boredom wasn't accompanied by quizzes. Precious daydreaming time remained unencumbered for one final week. Summer vacation had yet to loosen its grip. *Maybe teachers know we wouldn't be listenin' anyway.*

Friday afternoon finally came and giddiness filled the air. He, too, felt welling euphoria, having survived the initial week of the new school year yearning for the weekend like everyone else. Maybe by next week the routine would feel a bit more comfortable. Although sitting across the room, the clock suspended in the hallway beyond the window in the classroom door was perfectly visible and held his attention better than anything his teacher had said all week. He saw that all the kids who had a view of it watched it too. The teacher still spoke but it might as well have been Latin. Everyone moved to the edge of their seats like sprinters manning their blocks readying for a race. The signal to be set free was all that mattered at the moment.

It amused him. Kids flinched at every sound, ready to bolt. He decided that being the first out the door might be a dangerous place to be. One stumble could turn into a trampling disaster when every class converged on a single hallway at the same time.

Sitting next to the window had been a wonderful distraction. Ethan caught sight of every movement beyond the glass; cars on the street, birds on the wing swooping by, maintenance people, the yard man with his leaf blower-- even insects hovering over bushes. Bright sunshine begged him to come and be a part of fading summertime--a difficult time for an eleven year old, going on twelve, to be attentive to anything aside from personal pleasure.

The final bell rang.

Near-deafening cheers erupted.

The clumsy rush was on.

Ethan chose to sit for a while and watch a squirrel work on a pecan on the sidewalk outside. When the squirrel became uncomfortable, sensing prying eyes, it scurried away with its prize, leaving Ethan with nothing to watch and no reason to stay. Gathering his books, he noticed he was not the last one in the classroom. Rebecca Sanders had her nose close to a piece of paper, working on a doodle. Since he had to walk past her anyway, he thought it'd be polite to speak. "Hi, Rebecca. How was your first week?"

"Okay, I guess." She didn't look up.

"Make any friends?"

"Not really, but I haven't tried either."

She continued working on her picture, a house. "Is that where you live?"

"It was before we came to Plainfield. It was our home in Kansas City."

"It must have been special. You're working awfully hard on that picture of it."

She lowered her head even more, tilting away from Ethan's gaze.

"Are you okay?"

"Just go away," she muttered. "Please."

"Look Rebecca, I can--"

"Get outa here and leave me alone!"

Stunned by the attack, he stepped back. "Okay, okay...geez, I was just tryin' to be nice." He walked away, out of the room then trotting down the hall, outside, all the way to the buses lined up preparing to run their routes.

As he made his way down the narrow aisle of the crowded bus, he thought: *She's a doggone loony tune. Momma may have been right; the whole family might be nuts.*

He found Bubba who gladly squeezed a first grader into the window to make room for him. Ethan sat scrunched against his friend with his knees in the aisle. As he attempted to make sense of Rebecca's strangeness, he noticed Jessie and her boyfriend, Bobby Wells. They seemed to be engaged in a thinly controlled argument. The whispers sounded like strong hisses as they exchanged words he couldn't make out. When the bus stopped in front of the Well's house, Bobby jumped up and snapped, "I don't care, Jessie! Do whatever you gotta do...just don't make me part of it!" He stormed up the aisle and out the door, leaping to the ground without taking the steps. The driver ground the gears. The old yellow school bus shuddered and was again on the move.

After the crowd on the bus thinned, Ethan jumped forward and alighted on a seat behind his sister. "What's wrong with Bobby?"

"It's none of your business, twerp."

"Boy, he was sure mad about something. What happened?"

"Shut up, Ethan! Just shut up!"

Ethan recoiled, sitting back hard. The sudden outburst left him speechless. He went back to sit with Bubba. "Do me a favor and smell my breath."

"Shoot no. It probably smells like chicken crap. Why're ya askin' me to do such a stupid thing anyway?"

"People want to scream at me today and I wanna know why. It's gotta be my breath. I sure haven't done anything to deserve it."

The bus stopped in front of the Lee farm. Jessie dashed off first and ran nonstop up the long rutted dirt driveway. Ethan stepped off and stood, wondering what to do next. The bus moved on and the sound died away as it disappeared in a cloud of dust. He watched it for a time, not eager to be home just yet or anywhere adults might be ruling things. Dropping his backpack, he picked up a handful of small dirt clods from outside the nearest cultivated cotton row that bordered the driveway. He chunked them one by one at a small horned toad. The warm breeze that brushed his left side suddenly swirled and struck him from the opposite side and was noticeably cooler. The horned toad didn't seem to like the sudden change and sprinted away. It felt nice. Ethan drew a deep breath of the fresh northerly breeze. Suddenly, he had visions of holidays in the months ahead, putting a smile back on his face.

He picked up his backpack and continued on to the house, noticing his father again crouched in a cotton row, checking maturing bolls that were turning dark and almost ready to reveal the fluffy white cotton inside. But this time his father had a disturbed look on his face. Approaching the backdoor of the house, Ethan kept an eye on him.

Suddenly, his father yanked his cap off and threw it to the ground. He was angry; but why?

Bursting through the back door, Ethan stopped by the kitchen. "Momma, what's wrong with Daddy? He sure looks mad."

"Never you mind," just go wash up for supper."

"Well, why would he--"

"Do as I say, Ethan!"

He stopped cold with his mouth still open. The remainder of that sentence lay like soured vomit, left with no choice but to swallow it. He went on to his bedroom. "What's wrong with people today? What the heck is the deal?" he mumbled.

Later, he felt tension at the supper table. There was no conversation beyond a request to pass the beans or for more iced tea. He saw strained faces on his mother, father and sister. He couldn't stand the quiet. "Cotton is sure loadin' up good with big bolls. It looks great, doesn't it, Daddy?"

Sid didn't look up. "Eat your supper."

Thinking he may have chosen a sensitive subject, he decided on another. "How'd you like that cool air. Did y'all feel it when it came in?"

His father slammed a fist on the tabletop. "Dang it, Ethan! Be quiet and eat!"

That was the final straw. Once again a monster sat at the supper table and his family refused to acknowledge it--a dividing line separating problems from solutions. Ethan couldn't control his face, contorting and tearing. His father's outburst crushed him. He ran from the house crying. He didn't understand why so much anger had been directed at him all day.

Darkness had overtaken the light of day. The only remnant was a thin ribbon of orange in the western sky. The air had continued to cool and brought on shivers as he sat on an overturned fifty-five gallon drum just beyond the back yard. *Why does everyone hate me?* He cried.

After a short time, he heard the squeak of the screen door. Through watery eyes, he saw his father come out, silhouetted by light spilling from behind. Ethan didn't care. He was determined to keep his mouth shut and save himself from more attacks and more heartache.

Sid sat beside him, quiet for a moment. Then, "It's gettin' chilly."

Ethan didn't speak.

"Even the lightning bugs seem to have found warmer places. I don't see any. Do you?"

Still, Ethan said nothing.

"I don't even hear crickets. Do you hear any?" Sid looked to Ethan, trying to fire up a conversation.

Ethan refused to talk, sniffing and wiping tears from his face.

"Look, Ethan…I came out here to apologize. I shouldn't have blown up like that. I wasn't angry with you, but you sure have a right to be angry with me. Forgive me?"

Ethan looked at his father but still didn't talk.

"Your mother and I were hit with two things today that might grow into big problems."

One thing about being eleven years old is the inability to contain curiosity very long. "What things?" He sniffed.

"For one, this cool air you thought felt so good may turn into a frost tonight. If it's cold enough long enough it could be a killing freeze. If that happens, not only would we not get the late frost we hoped for, it'd be the earliest frost on record. It'd lock those cotton bolls closed. They'd never open...in other words a total crop loss."

Flatly, "It won't freeze."

"What makes you so sure?"

"I feel it here," he said, pointing to his stomach.

"Oh," his father said, smiling. "They call that a gut feeling."

"Yeah…one of those."

His father seemed to have more difficulty putting the next problem into words. He made one false start then another. Finally, "And on the other matter, let me just say you might be an uncle before your twelfth birthday."

Ethan crinkled his nose. "I don't understand."

"Your sister might be pregnant. We don't know yet."

Ethan's eyes grew large. "A baby?" He suddenly and clearly realized everything. "You were handing me a sack with a wildcat in it. That's all you were doing."

"What in the world do you mean by that?"

"It's nothing." He smiled through the tears, rubbing his red eyes. He thought about Jessie's angry response on the bus, how his mother snapped at him and his father's outburst. It all made sense. It was fear of things they couldn't control, having nothing to do with him or anything he said. "Rebecca," he blurted.

"What about Rebecca?"

"I need to talk to Momma." He jumped from his perch on the barrel and ran to the house throwing open the screen door. "Momma, weren't you going to the Sanders' house tomorrow?"

"That's the plan. I'm starting to bake the cakes right now. Why?"

"Can I go with you?"

"I don't see why not."

With a balled fist of determination, he pumped the air on the way to his bedroom. *This time it won't be so easy to make me leave, Rebecca Sanders. You can hand me all the bagged up wildcats you want to, I'm not gonna budge.*

Chapter Fifteen

"Did someone shoot at ya?"

"I hope not," Sid said dropping the newspaper into his lap with a noisy rustle. "What are you talking about?"

"Well, what did you mean when you said that you dodged a bullet?"

Reclining in his favorite chair, the foot support snapped up and he laughed.

Ethan came to his side. "What's so funny?"

"It's only a figure of speech, Ethan. The temperature fell below the freezing mark of thirty-two degrees last night…that was the bullet. It stayed there for about half an hour…that was dodging it. It didn't stay cold enough long enough to do any lasting damage to the cotton plants. That bullet only grazed us with a light frost…no damage done."

"Told ya so."

"Yes you did," his father said, and paused. Then came the now-familiar look of wonder.

Ethan dreaded that look. He figured someday, his daddy or momma might actually begin asking questions that he might have the answers to but would be forced to lie to keep a promise. That possibility scared him. But most of the things he told his father he didn't understand himself and only realized the reasons after the fact. What he did understand was that he was sworn to say nothing about the source of his wisdom.

His father patted him on the shoulder then smiled. "So far this season you're batting a thousand." The smile faded when Jessie walked by the living room door. He became fidgety in his recliner. "At least that's one piece of good news. Who knows, maybe we'll get more before the day's over." The hopeful sound in his voice trailed away.

Ethan watched his father's mood go cheerless, burying his nose back in the newspaper from where he'd emerged. A glimmer of optimism had surfaced concerning this year's crop, but a problem with potentially longer lasting consequences overshadowed it. Jessie walking by was a stark reminder of that.

His mother breezed into the living room. "Are you ready to go, Ethan?"

He stood for a moment, staring at the back of the newspaper that shielded him from his father's mood. He worried, wanting to say something cheerful, hopeful. Nothing came to him. "Well, I guess I'd better go."

All he heard was an unintelligible grunt from the other side of the paper.

"See ya." He trotted off to help his mother carry one of the cakes to the car.

Faye was on a mission to soothe her conscience and welcome a new family to town. Ethan was on his own quest. While his momma got to know Pamela Sanders, he was planning to figure out what made Rebecca Sanders tick.

On the way to town, Faye became apprehensive. She chattered. "I hope we're doing the right thing. I mean, what if we only anger her? What if I come off looking and sounding like a small town busybody? I don't want her thinking that way."

He knew his momma sincerely wanted to make a good impression; besides church on Sunday, this was one of the few times he saw his momma with her blonde hair not in a ponytail but hanging below her shoulders with sheen to it. And she wore a neatly pressed white blouse over a blue skirt. Her makeup was fixed perfectly. Ethan wanted to say something to make her feel better about her plan but she wouldn't stop talking long enough for him to speak. After a few failed attempts, he just listened and nodded.

The address of the Sanders home was a section of Plainfield they seldom visited--large expensive homes in a gated community. "What do you think?" she asked, as they drove past the guard gate.

"I think you should have put more icing on the cake."

Faye laughed. "Thanks. I needed that."

The exclusive neighborhood in a predominantly middle class farming community was appropriately small. There wasn't much money to be made farming or running businesses that catered to farmers. Finding the right address was a snap. Faye steered into a driveway behind a familiar SUV, dwarfing their aging sedan. "Ready or not..." she said then got out. "Just leave that other cake in the car."

"Sure." *Why would I want to mess with Mary Winn's bribe?* He ran ahead of his mother to the front door then waited for her to catch up, holding his finger near the doorbell button. He started to ring it, but that finger rejoined the rest in his fist when he heard an angry voice coming from inside the house. He dropped his hand away from the button and put his ear to the door. He tried to determine who was speaking. It sounded like Rebecca's mother. She shouted, "We're not moving back to Kansas City! We can't! How many times do I have to tell you that? Quit whining and shut up!"

Ethan sucked in a deep breath and held it for only a second. Then released it in a whoosh, "Oh, well," he said and reached again for the button.

His mother had heard the angry words, too, fumbling with the cake and grabbing for his arm a fraction of a second late. He'd already punched the doorbell button. For better or worse the plan was in motion.

Ethan looked around to see his mother's eyes widen and thought, *did I mess up?*

The door yanked open with a whoosh. "What is it?" Mrs. Sanders snapped.

Ethan saw his mother's jaw go slack. "Hi... uh...my name is Faye Lee and this is my son Ethan," she stammered then quickly added, "He's in your daughter's class at school."

Rebecca stuck her head around a door down the hall.

Ethan saw her and waved.

She didn't respond, withdrawing back into the room.

"I'm sorry," Mrs. Sanders said. "It's hectic around here." She attempted a smile. "I'm a little scatterbrained today. I can't seem to get anything done."

Faye held the cake out. "I baked a German chocolate cake for you and your family. I hope you like it."

The kindness seemed to touch her. She took it. "Please, come in. I'll start a pot of coffee. My name is Pamela." She extended a trembling hand to his momma.

Once Mrs. Sanders returned from the kitchen to join them in the living room, she wrung her hands, twirled her long uncombed auburn hair and continually straightened furniture or fluffed pillows. She wore sweat-bottoms beneath an oversize t-shirt with a faded "Support R.I.F." slogan emblazoned across its front. It appeared as though the get-up might have been her pajamas and she hadn't dressed yet, and here it was almost noon on Saturday.

When insignificant tasks ran out to keep her hands busy, she nibbled on her fingernails. The woman couldn't relax. She laughed at everything. He had no idea what she thought was so funny; most of the conversation was boring, certainly not funny. She'd laugh in short bursts after nearly every comment she made. Although she was very pretty, her face was drawn with dark circles under her eyes. She appeared older than his momma. Yet he figured they had to be about the same age, maybe even younger. After a time she went back to the kitchen to pour coffee.

"I must admit," Faye called out from the living room, "The cake is an offering to ease my guilt because I failed to introduce myself at school registration a couple of weeks ago."

Before his mother finished the statement, Rebecca marched through the living room. She paid him and his mother no mind, as though they weren't even in the room, eyes fixed on the kitchen. She meant business--of some sort. No sooner had she disappeared around the corner than an argument broke out between her and her mother. This time it was a little more subdued, if no less intense. It didn't seem to net Rebecca any headway. She stormed back through. Still, she said nothing in recognition of their presence.

Mrs. Sanders returned. "Please forgive us," she said, "Rebecca and I can't seem to agree on anything since her father died."

"I'm sorry. I didn't know," Faye said.

106

"Neither of us is handling it very well. It'll take time. I'm trying best I can to hold us together until we both regain our equilibrium in this crazy world." She glanced to Rebecca's bedroom door. "I just hope when we do get through it, Rebecca and I can heal our differences. I can't imagine not being friends with my oldest daughter."

"I don't mean to pry, but would you mind telling me what happened?" Faye asked.

"Paul was to have been the new manager at the Bower County Grain Elevator. He hadn't even begun the job." She paused. "The explosion took him." She pulled a tissue from a box on the end table. "He was so excited. He bought this house even before the one in Kansas City had sold. I quit my job and came down here to join him." She daubed tears and sat on the sofa. She kept to the edge, as if she might jump and run at any moment.

She took a deep breath. "After the funeral in Kansas City, I tried to get my old job back, but it was already filled. So, moving back was not an option. The house there had sold quickly; Paul and I signed the contract and the deal was done in a couple of weeks. The housing market here is awful on homes in this price range. Fate brought us here and is apparently going to keep us here."

She rose and turned again toward the kitchen. "So, Rebecca, the twins and I are living on life insurance until I can find a job." She glanced over her shoulder. "We'll be downgrading our lifestyle very soon." Her eyes did a dance of darting glances around the house. She sighed. "It'll be tough. I'm struggling to get Rebecca onboard with it."

Guilt was obvious on his mother's face. Her misplaced opinion of this woman who was simply trying to cope bothered her terribly. As the conversation progressed, it also lightened. His mother offered to help with a job search. As a lifelong resident of the area she knew everyone worth knowing, even offering to keep Rebecca and the twins whenever Mrs. Sanders needed to interview for jobs or just needed downtime to recharge her emotional batteries. Pamela Sanders had gone from pariah to friend-becoming.

Yep, it's just a matter of how you look at things.

Since the conversation between his mother and Mrs. Sanders didn't include him, he began looking for opportunities to break away and find

Rebecca. He had business of his own to tend to and was committed to taking care of it on this visit. As the women chatted, they discovered a number of points in common. That's when Ethan saw his opportunity. He slipped away.

Gliding quietly over the plush carpet down the hall, he passed a series of closed doors. He thought about opening each one and looking but was fearful of being accused of snooping. As he walked, he thought he knew which door it was, but three in a row looked just alike. Then he came upon a door opened a crack. He peeked in and, sure enough, there was Rebecca. She was angrily stuffing clothes into a suitcase.

"Hi," he said, pushing the door open. "Whatcha doin'?"

"Go away, Ethan Lee, and leave me alone."

"No, I don't think I want to do that."

"Suit yourself."

Ethan pulled a small white wicker chair from the corner of the bedroom. He positioned it near her and sat then crossed his arms over his chest and quietly watched.

She tossed a folded pair of jeans onto the bed and glanced at him. "What're you lookin' at? You want to make me madder than I already am? Is that what you want?"

He grinned. "Now let me think; you is the answer to the first question, no covers the second and the answer to the third question is: that's not at all what I want."

"Then why are you looking at me like that?"

"I'm not sure. I think I'm watching a very sad girl who wouldn't recognize something good if it smacked her upside the head, or, if it came to see her and sat right next to her." He flashed a Cheshire cat grin.

"Oh, you're so full o' bull. I'm packing to move back to Kansas City. I don't belong here. I have no father here and I have no friends here." Then reality hit. She'd have no father back home in Kansas City either. Her choice of words came crashing in. She shoved the open suitcase across the bed. The contents spilled onto the floor on the opposite side of it. She fell onto the bed and cried. "Go away. Just leave me alone."

"I can't do that."

She looked through teary eyes at him for the first time. "What do you mean, you can't?"

"I mean friends don't leave friends feeling like you do. I may not be able to change how you feel, but I can be here if you need me. You don't have to be alone ya know."

"Friends? Are you saying you're my friend?"

"Yep, that's exactly what I'm sayin'." He leaned back in the chair and laced the fingers of both hands behind his head, committed to staying for the duration.

She held a bland stare on him, clearly disarmed--in a quandary over his confident refusal to leave. Like a patient gentleman he crossed his legs and laid his hands in his lap holding an unwavering smile.

In fits and starts she rolled over and sat on the edge of the bed. Then, in a sudden spurt, she leaped up and ran to him, hugging his neck with such force that the chair went over backwards. Ethan's legs flew up as they tumbled onto the floor, sprawling across the overturned chair. Still, she held tight to his neck. "Thank you," she wailed. "You don't know how much I need a friend."

Thinking she may have been hurt, "Are you okay?"

She hugged him harder then gasped for breath, all the while soaking the shoulder of his shirt with streaming tears. "I'm just happy I have someone to talk to that's not my mother."

"So," he said with an exaggerate Texas drawl, "you're crying because you're *happy*? Is that it?"

"Yeah."

"I think I'm looking forward to the day you're not sad or happy. I just want to know what you look like when you're not crying."

Chapter Sixteen

Ethan lay in bed Sunday morning already dreading Monday. *Weekends are so darned short.* He counted the weeks until school would let out for the summer--too many to keep up with in his head. Approaching midmorning, the sun streamed at a high angle through the window. He thought of no good reason to be in a hurry to get out of bed and scanned the stuff in his bedroom--posters, toys, a tall case of shelves loaded with a clutter of model cars and planes--reminders of good times that had no connection to school. His mind suddenly clicked over to Rebecca. *Why do I think so much about her? I barely know her.*

"Ethan, get out of bed," came his mother's muffled call from another part of the house. "Are you just going to sleep 'til dinnertime?"

"I'm awake," he yelled but didn't move. Thoughts of Rebecca kept him occupied and not something he cared to interrupt just yet. Finally, he came to the conclusion he shouldn't show too much interest in her while at school. Classmates might start talking. If a buzz began, teasing wouldn't be far behind. *I don't want to ignore her though.* He sighed then frowned puzzling over the situation.

His father flung open the bedroom door. "Hop out of bed, hotshot, you have a lot of chores to do before dinner and your momma's fixin' fried chicken today." His father drew a broad grin. "I don't think you want to be late for that, because I promise ya, I'll have no problem eatin' your share."

"No sir." He jumped up and grabbed his favorite well-worn, threadbare faded blue jean cutoffs. Momma's fried chicken, mashed potatoes, gravy and biscuits could always put a spring in his step.

Ethan did the same chores every morning. He needed no instructions. He grabbed a bucket hanging from a picket on the backyard fence. Into the barn he marched and poured it full of chicken feed from the bag then stepping lively but awkwardly, toted the heavy bucket to the chicken coop. He dumped it into a long narrow trough. The birds crowded his feet. Shoving them away with the side of his foot, they squawked and flapped disapproval. He then dragged in a garden hose and filled the self-watering barrel. He then checked off that chore and moved on. The heavy ammonia smell of droppings covering the bottom of the coop reminded him it wouldn't be long before his father would have him scoop it out and spread it over the garden. He stayed in the moment, refusing to worry about future chores. Closing the coop door, Ethan left the unpleasant aroma behind.

The sun had moved higher in the sky. It was already warming up. The afternoon would likely be a scorcher--a little strange since the ground had been dusted in frost yesterday morning. He'd heard his father say, "That's Texas weather for ya," hundreds of times after abrupt weather changes. This year his father hoped for a long Indian summer.

On his way to the barn to pull a bale of hay and scatter it for the cows, he saw his father in that familiar pose, crouched in a cotton row, checking cotton plants loaded with unopened bolls as if that might, somehow, make them open a little quicker.

After he'd fed the cows and watered the fall garden of turnip greens, pumpkins and squash, he took off like a race walker toward the house, heel to toe, rolling his rear-end all the way. Even before he made it to the back yard, the smell of frying chicken just about lifted him off his feet. Waiting another hour for dinner was more than he could bear. "Momma," he shouted coming through the door, "If I help, can we eat early? I'm starving."

"Sure. Wash up and set the table."

The Lees had family meals together often, but busy schedules sometimes made that impossible during the week. Sunday was different. The rule was understood and mandatory; the family would sit together for Sunday dinner, no exceptions. It was darned near a sacred event--something kind of church-like about it.

Faye volunteered to say grace. Any other day that might have been unusual. She did so because she wanted to ask a special blessing on the Sanders family. Also out of character, Ethan repeated, "Amen," in a loud, definitive voice when she finished.

All of his mother's hard work was not wasted. The table was cleaned of food in short order. He thought he detected a slightly disgruntled look on her face. "Great dinner, Momma. That was so darned good, I think I could eat another whole bird by myself."

His mother beamed. That proved it; she believed the meal should have been lingered over a while longer. He also realized when a person is that good at something, perfection is viewed as normal and expected. And, by his way of thinking, his momma was darned near a perfect cook.

As traditional as Sunday dinner was, so happened to be the Sunday nap. Ethan lay on the sofa in a cool living room with one eye on a pre-season Dallas Cowboy football game. He became drowsy. It was an extraordinarily relaxed feeling brought on by a full belly, feeling cozy and protected--nothing to do and nowhere to be. He lazily glanced around the room as his father read the paper, his mother stitched a frayed pair of pants and Jessie quietly thumbed through a medical self-help book. *I bet she's reading about babies.* After his father had told him the news about his sister's problem, no one in the family had spoken of it again. But he was certain his mother added a silent prayer after the dinner blessing, pleading to God that his sister would not be pregnant.

Jessie had been quiet and obedient since the day she felt obligated to break the news of how her life could abruptly and dramatically change, apparently believing that suffering the pain of admission early might lessen problems later on. He figured that was pretty good reasoning. She might be doing some praying, too. As he stared at her, his eyelids became heavy then fluttered.

He dozed, drifting into a sound sleep.

112

Ethan suddenly found himself standing beneath his favorite tree, the big cottonwood hanging over the bend in Meandering Creek, providing cooling shade from the late summer heat. He wondered how he'd gotten there. He heard a rustle of leaves that didn't sound like wind then looked up to see the young man sitting on that precariously small limb again. The stranger didn't seem concerned about balance, gently swinging his crossed ankles back and forth, arms folded loosely over his chest, appearing quite pleased for some reason. He was smiling. "Am I dreaming?" Ethan asked.

"Yes, you are."

"Figures. You showed up too fast."

He looked around at the surroundings and wondered aloud, "Why does everything seem super real?"

"Super real?"

"Yeah. Everything looks like it should, only…better. The trees are greener, the sky is bluer, the water is clearer. In fact everything is perfect."

"That's because in a dream it is perfect. Your mind is painting a picture of the way it should look in your perfect world." The young man lifted off his perch, floating to the ground in front of Ethan, landing as gently as a butterfly.

"Hey, how'd you do that?"

"That's the neat thing about dreams. We can do anything that our minds don't put limitations on. What you see is only limited by the length, breadth and depth of your imagination. This is your favorite diving rock, so dive off of it…but don't go into the water. Go on, give it a try."

"You're crazy. If I dive off this rock, I'll get my good clothes wet. Momma'll whack my butt if I do."

"You see, right there, that's a limitation you're putting on yourself. Have I ever lied to you?"

"No."

"Okay then. There's nothing to be afraid of, and that's the truth."

"But everything seems so real. I feel the heat of the sun and the breeze across my face…" He crouched and slid his hand over the surface of the stone surface he stood upon. "…Even the hard coolness of this rock."

"Well, I did have a little to do with that. I needed your dream to be exceptionally vivid so you wouldn't forget it."

113

"Why?"

"First things first. Jump off this rock but don't hit the water."

"I've already told you...that's impossible."

"Do you know what faith is?"

"Sort of."

"Just so you're clear on it, faith is deeply believing something is true without having to experience it with any of the physical senses. Just because you can't touch it, hear it, smell it, feel it or see it, doesn't mean it's not so." The young man held his hands to his back. "Now jump off the rock. But before you hit the water, change your destination. Think about not wanting to be wet. Think, instead, about flying, about going up and coming back to stand on top of this rock, almost anything except hitting the water."

"I'm not sure why I should trust you, but something is telling me I should."

"There ya go, that's faith."

Ethan had dived off this rock hundreds of times. Like always, he held his breath and took a two-step running start. I'd better not get wet or my momma's gonna kill me. Once airborne, Ethan immediately knew something was different. He felt wind pushing him from beneath. It can't be wind. It feels like something soft is pushing me. Without effort, his fall reversed. He soared upward. A sudden rush of exhilaration overtook him. He squealed with delight, realizing he had control. He maneuvered his body one direction then another-- left, right, up, down. Ethan swooped low near the water's surface swishing his finger through it, licking the drops from the digit. He had no idea water from the old creek could taste so sweet. Arching his body, he shot straight up. Higher and higher he went. Wind pushed his hair back. He felt the air splitting around him, making way. Looking down he saw the young man from this lofty vantage point. He was looking back at Ethan with a genuinely happy smile. The young stranger, hands on hips, looked like Peter Pan. But it was Ethan who felt like the child that never had to grow up. The young man laughed with delight right along with Ethan--no doubt relishing the joy of witnessing unbridled bliss. After a time, Ethan came to rest upon his favorite diving rock alongside the young stranger. He examined his hands, arms, legs, feet, his whole body, as if he looked at them for the first time. He still felt a tingling rush in the pit of his stomach.

"Ethan, I have something important for you to remember: Your destiny and your future will always be in your control as long as you have faith in yourself, but your family

should be the center of it all." As gently as he had descended from the tree, the young man now floated up and back. "This should become part of who Ethan Lee is. Understand?"

"I guess so."

"Forevermore, my little friend." The young man grew smaller, drifting backwards beyond the cottonwood, away from the line of chinaberry trees--past all of it, but strangely, Ethan couldn't see the cotton fields he knew should be a little farther out from the creek, only drenched brilliance. "One last thing," the stranger said as he was fading away, "your sister is not pregnant."

"She's not gonna have a baby? Really? Is that what you said?" He became elated. "She's not pregnant. That's great! She's not..." A strange sensation overtook him. Something had changed. The words from his mouth didn't feel the same. The creek, the rock, the cottonwood--everything disappeared.

He opened his eyes. His father held the newspaper in his lap and stared at him. His mother was frozen in mid-stitch on the pants she mended. And Jessie looked at him with a silent question on her face too. He saw that the football game had jumped from the middle of the third quarter to near the end of the fourth. He lay on his side, mouth dry, swirling his tongue, swallowing hard and saw the darkened patch of drool on the sofa cushion. He glanced again at their stares. "What are y'all lookin' at?"

"Well, speaking for myself, I'm looking at a very strange little brother," Jessie said. She slapped the medical book shut. "But I hope you're right." She jumped up and left, apparently not wanting to participate in a conversation about it should her mother and father care to continue what he'd been babbling about in his sleep.

He watched his mother's eyes follow his sister out of the room. He wondered whether he should be feeling bad about inadvertently bumping a still-gaping wound, inflicting pain all over again. He sat up and rubbed the sleepy burn from his eyes and saw that his father and mother no longer looked at him but, instead, one another. The wonder in their faces contained questions he didn't have answers to. *Well this is a fine how-do-you-do. Now they all think I'm crazy.* He yawned and stretched. *I bet he wanted me to say that out loud.*

He heard an excited announcer and cheering from the television. The Cowboys scored. He fell over to finish his nap.

Chapter Seventeen

As it was turning out, school was not as evil as it could have been. Still, the week moved torturously slow--boredom riddled and at the bottom of his priorities--one more whole day before Saturday. Thursday was coming to a blessed end. He spent the last few minutes of the school day considering recent events as he doodled on his notebook.

A potential problem of suffocating proportions had lifted off the Lee family; moods had brightened. But it had taken time and didn't come easily. Not that it mattered now but Ethan was curious how his mother, father and Jessie figured out that she wasn't pregnant even before she went into Plainfield for her doctor's appointment Monday morning. But the mystery was less important than the news. He suspected that it had something to do with those times she transformed from difficult older sister into a real witch. He never knew why. It just seemed that every few weeks she'd become agitated for no apparent reason and he was usually the target of her discontent.

He drew a picture of a small devil, complete with horns, pointy tail and pitchfork, his interpretation of his sister during those times. *Yep, that's how she looks all right...at least once a month.* Jessie announced to their parents that dating would not be an issue for a long time to come.

He checked the clock suspended from the wall outside the classroom--five minutes to go.

Ethan was proud of his mother. She'd kept her word to Pamela Sanders to ease her burden of transition to a new community as a single mother forced upon her by the death of her husband and Rebecca's father. While Ethan established a relationship with Rebecca, his mother offered to keep her and the twins from Thursday after school until Sunday morning. Mrs. Sanders accepted because she'd been granted an interview for a job to manage a small group of convenience stores in the Plainfield area but must travel to the home office in Abilene for it. This allowed time to research the local market, perfect her resume and drive to Abilene at a leisurely pace for a Friday afternoon interview. She could answer questions backed by strength of knowledge without worrying about the safety of her children.

Because his mother had told him so, it was a solid fact. To tell a lie just wasn't in her although bribery seemed to be an acceptable form of getting things done--like baking a German chocolate cake in exchange for information.

He abruptly stopped drawing little pictures and geometric designs on his notebook cover. It occurred to him that garnering information by bribing Mary Winn with a cake wasn't quite right, but it wasn't quite wrong either. He wondered about that and found himself in a quandary. It brought to mind the stranger's explanation about the age of innocence and how decisions would become harder to make because of those "gray areas." *Is this one of those?* He couldn't say yes and he couldn't say no. He again checked the clock--two minutes until the final bell.

Ethan looked forward to knowing Rebecca better. The short conversations at school attracted teases and gossip. Ethan worried about what people thought and how his relationship with Rebecca would be viewed. He tried to keep the scale balanced between what they thought and how he actually felt and, at the same time, not make Rebecca feel neglected. A girl as a *friend* was not the same thing as having a *girlfriend* but trying to explain that to other eleven year olds just wouldn't work. *She's just a friend...I guess.* But the word *girlfriend* resided comfortably in his thoughts.

The final bell broke the silence and startled him although expecting it. The student body was unleashed on the world. A stampede of pounding feet created noise that whoops and hollers had trouble rising above. Streaming and screaming, they shoved one another into the sweet freedom of the outdoors and on to the waiting buses. The race for the best seat was no less intense, all pushing to congregate within cliques. Ethan imagined cattle crowded and prodded onto rail cars. But no electric prods were necessary here--nothing could slow them down.

Rebecca sat near the front and offered him a seat. "No thanks. I'll go on back and sit with Bubba." Glancing over his shoulder, marching to the rear of the bus, he saw that his refusal upset her. The twins plopped down next to her without invitation. She didn't look happy. *I hope I don't goof around and mess things up.*

He slapped Bubba on the shoulder and shoved him over. Ethan comfortably fell into good-natured roughhousing, glancing at Rebecca often. Her younger brother and sister, the twins, Pete and Patty, annoyed her. Ethan saw motherly discipline from Rebecca. She stabbed the air between them with a stern finger telling them something he couldn't hear, but the younger children responded with pouty faces. He swelled with admiration of her.

He thought it strange because his own sister, Jessie, spent more time trying to get rid of him than telling him how to behave. It must have something to do with losing her father.

Bubba apparently didn't care for Ethan's loss of focus and smacked him upside the head, bringing him back to the scuffle at hand. It ended when the bus stopped to let Bubba off at his house.

Ethan followed him to the front of the bus and sat in the empty seat behind Rebecca. "See ya Monday, Bubba."

Bubba looked back and grinned. "Yeah, we'll pick up where we left off Monday morning."

"You betcha."

Few students remained on the bus. He now felt safe striking up a conversation, tapping Rebecca on the shoulder. "How was your day?"

"Fine," she said with a snippy chill in her voice.

"We'll be home soon."

She kept facing forward and said crisply, "Okay."

Ethan realized he'd hurt her feelings. Never being the one to walk away from a sensitive subject, "I'm really looking forward to having you for the weekend, so if I do or say anything you don't like would you let me know?"

She still didn't look back but he noticed her shoulder sink and her head relaxing forward. "I will."

Although there was no overt language of forgiveness, he sensed that she had forgiven him. She became chattier, talking about a particularly difficult pop quiz they'd had that day. They compared notes. Between reprimands of Pete and Patty's noisy behavior, she spoke freely until the bus approached the driveway to his house.

"Come on y'all." Ethan rose, moving up the aisle before the bus had stopped. "We're here." He leaped through the open bus door to the ground and waited for his guests to get off. Once everyone was out and the bus growing smaller in the distance, it was clearly a culture shock for three city kids unaccustomed to the awesome lack of noise accentuated by the fading rumble of the school bus. Ethan hadn't realized how something as simple as silence could be intimidating. Before today their only experience with country living was through the back window of a car. Now they were in the middle of it. The twins lost their verve and stood huddled together. They probably felt as though they'd landed on some obscure crossroads in the desert, up the road from nowhere and just south of no place.

"Wow," Rebecca said, "You guys shouldn't be bothered by noisy neighbors."

"I'm not sure we could hear our closest neighbors even if they used a big ol' bullhorn."

The twins crowded around Rebecca like frightened chicks to a mother hen. She pushed them away. "Come on guys. It'll be okay. Ethan's a good guy. He wouldn't let anything bad happen to us."

Ethan puffed with pride standing a little straighter and holding his head a little higher.

As they walked the long rutted dirt driveway toward the house, Rebecca said, "It's a beautiful farm." She walked with a bouncy step, turning towards him as she did. "What do you do for fun?"

"That's easy." He pointed across her to the slope leading down to a line of trees that stretched diagonally all the way across the farm, "Ya see those trees?"

"Yeah."

"That's Meandering Creek. See that cluster of trees?"

"Where?"

"Hold on a minute."

She stopped and he moved around behind her placing an outstretched arm over her shoulder to offer a line of sight. "Right there, that biggest cottonwood tree...ya see it now?"

"Oh yeah, how could I've missed that? It's huge."

"The creek takes a sharp bend and there's a deep pool of water right there. I spend all my free time there when it's warm outside. It's my private place. I swim there all the time."

"It sounds wonderful. Will you show it to me?"

"Sure, but not today. By the time we do homework and eat supper it'll be dark."

"Oh."

"I'll tell you what though; if it's warm Saturday, we'll go down together and swim all afternoon. How about that?"

Rebecca smiled and narrowed the gap between them as they walked. Ethan made a conscious effort not to drift away. The closer to him she walked, the better he felt. It was weird. "When we get to the house, drop your stuff and y'all follow me. I have chores to do, but they won't take long."

"You sure we won't be in the way?"

"Nah."

At his insistence, she and the twins followed him as he went about after-school duties. Rebecca disciplined the young ones often to stay away from animals and sharp objects, of which there were many of both. Each time she did, he stopped and patiently waited. Any other day, he'd be antsy to get it done and back to the house. This time, dreaded chores just didn't seem all that bad.

But Rebecca was becoming frustrated with her younger brother and sister. "I'm sorry. I know we're being pains and slowing you down."

"No problem. Really."

The annoyance didn't end with the chores; Pete and Patty made themselves at home--a little too much. He and Rebecca tried to do homework but interruptions were frequent. Almost constant reprimands of the two had little effect.

Ethan believed himself curious, but his need to know things couldn't compare to the insatiable curiosity of those two. *Those screeching yard apes are the nosiest kids I've ever seen.* He watched them snoop through everything, playing with delicate porcelain figurines and running dangerously close to small occasional tables covered with things easily broken. Rebecca tired. Watching after and chasing them down when necessary sapped her mood.

Ethan dropped his pencil, excused himself, and headed for the kitchen. "Momma, after supper would you watch the twins for a while? I think Rebecca needs time without them around."

His mother seemed to appreciate his concern. "Sure, sweetie."

As promised, after supper his mother called the two youngsters in to her.

As soon as the twins disappeared Ethan grabbed Rebecca's hand. "Come on, let's go outside."

His mother stepped back when she heard him and peeked into the living room where they had been doing homework. "It's getting dark. Stay close to the house."

Ethan guided Rebecca onto the front porch, a place he seldom visited. It was his mother and father's occasional domain. A porch swing and two rocking chairs were fixtures and had been as long as he could remember. It also happened to be where Faye kept a veritable jungle of potted plants, doting over them frequently.

Rebecca trotted to the swing, sat and shoved off. "Come sit beside me." She patted the slats next to her.

Ethan backed up and let it swing under him. He almost missed. They laughed.

As they watched the last ribbon of light change from pink to orange then blood red to indigo and finally blending with the rest of the night sky, they talked and kept swinging while listening to crickets and watching fireflies. The only light remaining happened to be the glow of a lamp filtered through white sheer curtains through the window next to the swing.

Eventually, things to talk about ran low but they continued swinging. After a time, Ethan glanced at her then quickly away. "Do you believe in ghosts?"

"Why? Do you?"

He sighed. "I'm not sure."

"What would make you ask such a question?"

Ethan had had very little trouble keeping the closely guarded secret of his friend's presence at the creek, until now. He wanted to confide in Rebecca, to tell her the whole story and was increasingly compelled to do so. *I've already asked the question, now what? Do I just take off and tell her and freak her out?* "You first," he said, "Do you believe in them or not?"

"Yes, I do."

Surprised, "You sure answered fast."

"Well, I just have faith they exist. That's all."

There's that word "faith". "Why so sure?"

"I believe my father is out there somewhere watching over us." She gazed into the darkness then up to the stars. "It…it helps to think so."

"I'm sorry. I didn't mean to make you sad."

"It's okay. You couldn't know it'd make me think of my father. Almost everything that crosses my mind makes me think of him though. It'll take a long time to get over it. Reminders are all around me all the time. I'm not so sure I'll ever be over it."

"Maybe you can start making some happy memories." He nervously tugged at his ear, glancing at her then looking away. But he couldn't keep his attention elsewhere and, again, looked at her. This time he held a gaze on her profile. "How about we work on that together…making some good memories I mean? Okay?"

She brushed a tear from her cheek. "I'd like that."

Ethan spent the rest of the evening toying with the notion of sharing his new friend with Rebecca. He couldn't seem to find the words or the right time.

Every way he thought of to tell her would make him appear as though he'd lost his mind. No way seemed like the right way. So he kept it to himself.

The front door creaked open. "Ethan, you and Rebecca come on in. It's time for bed," his mother said.

Lying in bed it roiled in his mind. He became committed to sharing it with her at some point--the commitment was not without uncertainty. *How? If I tell her about him and he refuses to show up, it's gonna make me look stupid. After school tomorrow and all day Saturday she'll be close. Maybe I'll get my chance.* He became excited at having her as the only other member of a very secret club. It occurred to him that if that guy turned out to be just a sneaky but ordinary young man, it might be a disappointment once Rebecca was onboard with it. Drowsy, he saw the star-filled moonless night sky through his bedroom window. *Those stars sure are extra twinkly tonight.* Sleep came swiftly.

Chapter Eighteen

Rebecca became comfortable within the Lee household environment. Ethan was proud of that. Friday evening, she talked incessantly. Going to the creek Saturday and swimming had become an obsession. She mentioned it often and hoped it would be a pretty day. Ethan enjoyed watching her transformation and thought her real personality had just now begun to emerge, probably closer to what she was like living in Kansas City. Getting away from her house and sad reminders seemed to be the right medicine at the right time.

From his bedroom where he and Rebecca had been playing games on the floor, he heard the weather report come on television. Rebecca responded first. She grabbed his hand and yanked him to his feet, pulling him into the living room, giggling and listening for one thing--the afternoon high temperature for Saturday. Late September was always a time the weather might go from hot to frigid in twenty-four hours but, so far, weather suitable for swimming seemed promising. Even the experts said nothing about cold weather anytime soon.

He grinned. "It's startin' to look like a darned good plan."

She clutched his hand with both of hers, shrugged her shoulders tight as a faint squeal of elation escaped through the broadest grin he'd ever seen on her.

Saturday morning, she eagerly helped with the chores, already wearing snug-fitting shorts and a tight t-shirt. Rebecca wasn't as tall or slender as his sister, Jessie, but she was also three years younger. She had long dark hair with some natural curl. To Ethan, it was the perfect combination. She pushed him to work faster. "Come on, Ethan, quit messin' around. Get that hay scattered and let's go."

He was just as eager but enjoyed watching her explosive excitement, the twinkle in her eyes and the glow in her cheeks. He purposely slowed, just so he could watch. "I *am* hurrying," he said, well aware he strained the truth. Even as he wrapped things up, he persisted in dawdling.

Rebecca pulled him along by the wrist. He pretended to be plumb tuckered out, like he was hindered by heavy weights on his feet, dragging his toes. He made her work for every step he took.

"Come on, come on, come on," she said, practically begging. Ethan began laughing. She slapped him on the stomach. "You're doing that on purpose." She pushed out a pouty lip.

They began to trot toward the creek across the end of the cotton rows and passed where his father knelt, pushing plants over to look at bolls that had begun to open, displaying the fluffy white cotton inside. "Lookin' good, huh Daddy?" Ethan shouted.

"It does for a fact." His father plucked an open boll and tossed it at Ethan.

Ethan stopped, picked it up and waved it in her face. "Just think, Rebecca, someday the socks you're wearin' might be made from this very boll of cotton." He sniffed it. "And it smells better than any ol' flower, too."

"Don't forget," his father said, "you promised a late killing freeze and we probably need another six weeks of warm weather with no rain. Can you handle that?"

"No sweat, Daddy. You've got it." He again began to trot.

Rebecca, following close behind, "What did he mean by 'you promised' a late killing freeze? It's not like you have control over things like that."

"It's sort of a family joke. I've made some pretty good guesses about things this summer. I think Momma and Daddy are a little spooked by it."

Ducking under a low hanging chinaberry limb, he held it back until Rebecca joined him on the bank of the creek. With a sweeping gesture toward the diving rock above the pool of water, "Ta-da! This is it. Whaddaya think?"

Rebecca was not disappointed. She slipped off her canvas deck shoes and wriggled her toes into the loose dry sand above the waterline, enjoying the sun-warmed feel. She took her time, studying everything--the creek, the deep pool, and that magnificent high diving rock. When her eyes settled on the lower jutting rock, she said, "That darned thing is so flat it looks like someone made it that way."

"Someone did make it that way...God." He feigned superiority, lifting his nose in the air. "And he made it just for me."

She backhanded him on the upper arm. "Silly." Her excitement clicked up a notch when she looked up. She pointed to the obvious king of the flora. "That tree is huge." She looked it up and down, shielding the filtered sun from her eyes.

"Yeah, it's my favorite...a big ol' cottonwood, best tree on the farm. It shades this whole swimmin' hole."

Rebecca's eagerness vanished. She now seemed to want nothing more than soak up the sight. She did a full three-sixty examination of everything. She then grinned and twirled. "This place is absolutely magical."

Ethan's breath hitched. "What do you mean by that?"

"I mean it's so beautiful it takes my breath away. That's all."

"Oh." *But why magical? Why that word?* "Hey, you wanna see something really cool?"

"Sure. What?"

"My ol' friend the catfish."

"Your what?"

"Come on I'll show ya." Ethan ran headlong into the water and swam a few feet until he realized he hadn't heard her hit the water.

Whirling around on the surface, he saw her testing it with her toe. "Oh come on, ya big sissy, dive in."

"I suppose you could've called me a lot worse." Holding her breath, she clumsily ran a few steps, lost her footing and fell face first with a splat.

He swam back and helped her up.

Rebecca's long auburn hair had suddenly become anything but attractive, plastered across her face. She sputtered and spit creek water.

He waited for her to regain composure. "Are you all right?" As he became comfortable that she was, he drew a catty grin then he laughed.

He turned and swam, guiding her over and down to that part of the diving rock below the waterline. He put his face in close, searching the underwater cleft, but ran out of air trying. He didn't see it anywhere. They shot back to the surface. As they huffed for breath, "I don't understand. That ol' catfish stayed in that crack all summer long. I wonder where he could be?"

"He's moved on, Ethan. All things have their season, including me," came the familiar voice.

Rebecca, still bobbing and paddling in a circle didn't seem startled at all by the abrupt voice. "Don't worry about it. It's okay," she said. That fish'll probably come back. Maybe it's just looking for something to eat."

Ethan didn't know whether to respond to Rebecca or to the voice. He stared at her, dumbfounded.

She noticed the strange look on his face. "What is it?" she asked. "Do I have something crawling on my face?"

"He shook it off. "No...nothing like that." As casually as he could, he looked around but saw no one. "Did you...by chance...hear somebody talking?"

"No."

"She could hear me if she wanted to," the voice said.

"How about now?"

"What in the world are you talking about? I don't hear anything but you."

Ethan pulled himself out of the water up onto the low jutting rock. He then helped Rebecca up to sit beside him. They sat, feet dangling in the water.

"Well...don't just sit there, talk to me," she said. "Are you hearing things?"

Dadgummit! This is embarrassing. Tightly pursing his lips and working his jaw muscles, he looked all around. Still, he saw no sign of the young man. He noticed uneasiness on her face. *I must look like a loony tune to her.*

"A loony tune, huh?" The voice said. "I don't mind if you tell her the whole story. We don't want her thinking you're insane...now do we?"

"Hey, I didn't say that out loud," he blurted. Only then did he realize Rebecca had no idea what he was talking about.

Her mouth fell open. Her look went from concern to startled. "Ethan Lee, you're scaring me."

He didn't look at her or respond to the comment, just kept glancing around.

"Don't be embarrassed," the voice said. "Just tell her the whole story. It'll be okay, I promise."

"I think...I want to go back to the house," she said and began to slide off into the water to swim back across the creek.

He grabbed her arm. "Wait." He took a deep breath. "I have something I need to tell you." As she settled next to him, he took swipes at the water with the tips of his toes and watched the radiating rings move outward from them. "First, you have to swear you're not going to think I'm crazy. Second, you're the only one that can know. You can't tell anyone. I haven't even told Bubba about it. Ya promise?"

"About what?"

"You gotta promise first."

Annoyed, "Okay, I promise."

"Remember the other night when I asked if you believe in ghosts, and you told me you did?" He glanced sideways at her.

She nodded.

"Well, I'm still not so sure I do, but a man has been comin' around to visit me here at the creek. He seems nice enough, but he has a strange way of knowing what I'm thinkin' and doing weird things like...disappearin'. At least, I think he is. Maybe he's just really good at hidin'. Anyway, I'm sorry that I scared you, but you gotta know that I'm pretty darned scared right now, too, because I just found out I can hear him and you can't. That's scarin' the bejesus out of me!"

Her eyes grew large. She scooted closer and whispered, "Can you see him now?"

"No. But he talked to me. That's what's spookin' me. You couldn't hear him."

"Ask her again if she has faith that her father is watching over her," the voice said.

Ethan snapped his head around, this way then that, still not seeing him.

"Did you just hear him again?" she asked.

He nodded. "Do you still have faith that your father watches over you?"

"Sure I do." She looked serious, but only for a second then laughed.

"What's so funny?"

Abruptly, she stopped laughing. "Oh, I'm not laughing at you. I thought it was funny that I was afraid you might believe I'm crazy if I *didn't* believe in ghosts, and you're afraid I'll think you're crazy if you *do*."

He felt a hand on his shoulder and looked up into the face of the young stranger. Then he noticed that her attention had shifted away. She looked up too.

"Hi," the young man said to Rebecca.

"Hi," she said.

"You can see and hear him, right?" Ethan asked.

"Don't be silly. Sure I can see and hear him. He's standing right there."

"Who are you?" she asked.

"Well, I was just a friend of Ethan's, but now, I'm a friend of yours too."

"What's your name?"

"I'll let Ethan tell you that?"

"Wait a doggone minute! I don't have a clue what your name is."

"You will," he said. He pushed them apart and sat between them on the rock.

"I have no idea who you are," she said, "But I'm not at all nervous. You don't scare me in the slightest."

"That's nice to hear," the young man said.

She smiled across him at Ethan and pointed an accusing finger. "But he did a pretty good job of scaring me about you."

The stranger looked at Ethan's embarrassed face. "Yeah, the boy can be a might skittish at times." He turned his attention back to her. "I don't like it when people manipulate others for the cheap thrill of watching them react...scaring them would be a good example of that."

She poked the young man's thigh with a fingertip. "You sure don't feel like a ghost."

He leaned over and poked her on the arm. "You don't either," he said. "What made you think I was a ghost? Did Ethan tell you that?" He put his hands on his hips and looked suspiciously at Ethan.

"Not exactly. He just told me you acted kind of strange."

"If acting strange was a prerequisite for being a ghost, this old world would be full of pretty frightening specters."

Rebecca burst into laughter and leaned across in front of the young man to Ethan, "He's right, you know."

Ethan's mild embarrassment went over the top and turned bright crimson. "Well...maybe. But he sure seems to know a lot of stuff he shouldn't."

"Really?" She turned to the young man. "Tell me something you shouldn't know but you do?" Rebecca grinned big now, believing it was all a game.

"I know that you and Ethan will know each other for a lifetime. So, it'd be a good idea to become really close friends now." The young man seemed to take on a softly smug appearance. "It'll make things a whole lot smoother down the road."

"Come on now," she said, cocking her head to a quizzical slant. "There's no way you can know that and no way to prove it."

"Only passage of time will prove me right...but it will." A Monarch butterfly alighted on his fingertip. He held it up and, as if about to kiss it, sent it on its way with a tiny puff of air. "You both will look back on this someday and remember it. This I promise."

Pushing back from the edge of the rock, the young man rose to his feet and dusted his hands. "Well, I've said enough for one day. It's been fun but I'd better not wear out my welcome."

"Wait a minute," Ethan said, "I have lots of questions."

"Ask anything you like," he said. "I'm in no hurry."

Realizing he had very little time, Ethan began to stammer, "Uh, where did you come from?"

"That way," he said, pointing behind him.

"That's not what I meant."

"Well, ask what you mean."

Rebecca watched, clearly amused.

"Okay. I don't want to know which direction you came from but *where* you came from," Ethan said.

"I came from where you'll be going to," he said.

"What?" Ethan blew a frustrated snort. "Are you saying you were up at the house before you came down here?"

The young man flippantly placed the point of his finger on his chin and then folded his arms over his chest, obviously just as amused as Rebecca. "No, that's not what I meant," he said. "But you know what? It fits. So let's go with that."

Ethan looked at Rebecca. "You see what I mean? I could ask this guy questions all day long and still not have a darned clue who he is or what he's doin' here…or where he came from."

Rebecca snickered at Ethan's frustration. "Don't get your cutoffs in a bunch, he's just playin' with you. She turned back to the young man. "Aren't you?" She looked up where he'd been standing.

He wasn't there.

She looked all around.

He was gone.

"Hey, where'd you go?" she called out.

It was Ethan's turn to smile. "Ya see what I mean. Poof! He just disappeared. Go ahead and look for him. I bet you can't find him anywhere."

As Rebecca walked from tree to tree, she looked behind each one, becoming intrigued. "What if he really is a ghost? What if he knows those things he's talking about?"

"Why do you think my family looks at me funny now? That guy tells me things then I pass the information along. So far, it's all been true. Spooky I tell ya...absolutely spooky."

Rebecca froze, wide-eyed. "He said we'd get married someday."

"No, he didn't. He said we'd know each other for a lifetime and we should become good friends."

"Right. That's what I said. We'll be getting married someday."

Chapter Nineteen

"Where's Daddy goin'?" Ethan rubbed the sleep from his eyes as he watched his father through the kitchen window drive away.

"We received a phone call earlier this morning that your grandma is sick. It looks serious," his momma said. "Right now she's at the retirement village in Ardmore and refusing to go to the hospital until Sid gets there. So, he's driving to Oklahoma to see her." She finished drying her hands on a cup towel and dropped it by the sink.

A look on his mother's face bothered him. He suddenly didn't feel sleepy anymore. Her expression was unusual--not sad, not happy. And she seemed focused on him. She gently wrapped her fingers around his upper arm, pulling him over to a chair then pushed him down onto it. She then pulled a chair around the end of the table and scooted it next to him and sat stroking his forearm and smiling, but in an odd bothersome way.

"What's the matter, Momma?"

"I don't think grandma Emily will be getting well this time." She brushed his cheek with a gentle sweep of her hand, pushed his lengthening hair aside then kissed him on the forehead.

Ethan didn't grasp the gravity of those words. "I wish she lived closer so I could see her more often. Maybe you can take me to town and I'll buy her a get-well card."

"I wish she lived closer, too. But, when your grandpa was alive and they retired, he was drawn back to his roots in Oklahoma." Faye pushed spread fingers through his unruly hair that had returned to a length in need of a comb. "You know, Ethan, people develop strong bonds with places. Sometimes, that bond can pull them back no matter how far away they get or how long they've been gone. Some people go to great lengths and overcome major obstacles simply to return to a place that holds special memories."

"Is that what grandma and grandpa did?"

"Yes, sweetie, it is. By their way of thinking they just went home. That's why they moved so far away. It had nothing to do with us. It was an urge they couldn't deny at their stage of life." With a livelier voice, "Someday, when you're off in Los Angeles or New York and a big movie star or head of a mega-million-dollar corporation, there'll come a time when this farm will tug at your heart to come home."

Ethan nodded. He certainly loved having a private place he could call his own and knew he'd never forget Meandering Creek. He began to think about what the young stranger had told him when they first met. When asked where he lived, he told Ethan, "Let's just say I live right here on this bend in Meandering Creek." The young man and his responses that seemed to avoid answers began to make more sense. Ethan believed that, somehow, his visits were connected to what his mother had just told him about special places. He just couldn't put it all together. *Why would Meandering Creek be special to him?*

She patted him on the leg. "Go wake Rebecca and the twins. Breakfast'll be ready soon." She returned to the kitchen.

It was a stark reminder that Rebecca would be going home today. Becoming deflated, he sighed. "Okay." He'd quickly grown accustomed to having her around, but not those rambunctious twins.

There was little talk around the breakfast table. Even Pete and Patty were bleary-eyed; elbows on the table, shoulders jacked and heads hung loosely, neither fully awake. Ethan studied and admired Rebecca's sleepy face. Then his eyes drifted back to her siblings. *I won't be missing you two…at all.*

His momma smiled at Rebecca. "Your mother called last night after you went to bed."

Suddenly, Rebecca looked more awake. "What'd she say?"

"First, she told me that she'll be here before noon to pick y'all up…"

Her face fell slack again. "Oh."

"…And, that she got the job."

Rebecca's smile popped. "Really?"

"Really. Best of all, it might be good enough that y'all won't have to move out of Plainfield, or even your new house for that matter."

Rebecca beamed.

The more radiant she became, the happier Ethan became. His smile stretched to match hers. *Boy, oh boy, oh boy.*

His smile faded when an image of his grandma flashed; sadness overlaid elation then it reversed when he looked at Rebecca. Guilt swarmed him. Something was terribly wrong in finding something to smile about so soon after hearing his grandma was sick. Still, he refused to think that his grandma was as bad off as his mother would have him believe.

After breakfast the good news opened new conversations; things that, until now, had been sidestepped as taboo but suddenly had been rendered harmless--things like the remainder of the school year. There'd been no agreement to avoid the subject, it just had been. Now, they laughed and chatted about holidays, parties and football games. A door had been opened to a brighter day. They laughed, ran and played. Ethan watched Rebecca bloom as she spoke of future things--happy expectations that began this very day.

The Sanders children greeted the arrival of their mother late in the morning with cheers and hugs. They climbed into the big SUV and began rolling down the driveway--too fast and too soon by Ethan's reckoning. Rebecca stuck her head out the window and hollered, "Thanks for *everything*. See ya Monday." She waved wildly with a smile as big as Texas. It set Ethan's heart on fire. He enthusiastically returned the wave, but even before his hand came down emptiness set in.

His mother draped her arm over his shoulder while she still waved with the other. "Rebecca's turning into a pretty good friend, isn't she?"

"Yeah. I guess she is."

"Does Bubba have anything to worry about?"

Shocked, he looked at her.

She bore a mischievous grin.

"Oh, no," he said stepping out from under her arm. "Bubba's my pal."

His mother said nothing more, just gave him that knowing look she was so famous for.

"At least I don't think so," Ethan said. He walked away, tangled in a notion he'd never considered before, until his mother pointed out that while he was with Rebecca he didn't seem to care about seeing Bubba. He shoved his hands deep into the pockets of his frayed denim cutoffs, walking barefoot to the edge of the yard where the cotton rows began. He sauntered, thinking. *I do feel bored all of a sudden. I never feel this way when Bubba stays over then leaves.* Coming to no conclusion over the odd flutter in the pit of his stomach, he looked and saw that he'd walked nearly all the way down to the creek.

Hands still stuffed deep in his pockets, his eyes outlined his favorite place, the big cottonwood tree, the diving rock, the row of chinaberry trees, as disjointed thoughts filled his head--things he wished would come together as something he could understand but, for now, just paraded in a random string of images that didn't seem to follow any order. *The stranger said I'd know Rebecca for a lifetime.* He tossed his hands into the air. *Why can't I figure this out, am I just stupid?*

It was calm and warm but comfortably so. He dropped down between two rows of cotton. It was easy to hide there now that the cotton stalks were shoulder-high. He again pretended he was a giant looking in on a forest and all its inhabitants; a fantasy he never tired of. He watched a ladybug search for the perfect aphid snack. A worm crawled over an open boll of cotton. The green looper fascinated him. "You missed your chance, little fella. That cotton's not fit to eat now…kinda tough and dry, I'd say. Why in heck are you still around this late in the year?" As he continued his examination of the world beneath the cotton leaf canopy, he heard a sound like wind blowing through leaves. He pushed himself up above the cotton stalks and looked toward the creek, the only place the sound could have come from. He didn't see anything unusual. It appeared calm there too. As he began to rejoin his make-believe world, he heard it again. This time he watched the uppermost leaves of the trees bordering the creek sway with a particularly hard gust of wind. He jumped up and trotted to the creek bank to investigate, but when he arrived he discovered no wind there either. "What in the world..."

"I'm glad you answered my call," the voice said.

"I didn't. I just thought it was strange the wind was blowing here and not up there." He pointed back to where he'd walked from.

"Like I said, I'm glad you answered my call."

"Huh?"

"Never mind, it's not important. Would you give a message to your grandmother for me? You'll have a chance this evening. I'd sure consider it a huge favor?"

"I guess so." Ethan's brow pulled down. "How do you know I'll have a chance to talk to her?"

"Just a feeling; I want you to be prepared in case you do." He remained out of sight.

"What's the message?"

"First, don't miss the chance to tell her you love her. Okay?"

"Okay."

"Secondly, tell her don't be scared and not to worry, Tater will be waiting."

"Tater? You mean potato, don't you? And why would a potato be waiting?"

"Not potato, silly...Tater; it's not a some-thing, it's a some-one. And he's not as smart as you're going to be. He missed his chance to tell her that he loved her, but now he's waiting to show her the way."

"The way where? Geez, man, I have a book of riddles easier to understand than you." He looked all around. "Aren't you going to come out and show yourself?"

"I can't," the voice said.

"Why not?"

"It's that pesky age of innocence thing."

"Oh yeah." It then struck him, "Wait a minute, I haven't kissed a girl yet."

"No, but your thoughts and feelings are equivalent. You're developing complex questions about relationships, friendships and your future. You're squeezing me out."

"I don't mean to."

"It's inevitable."

"I think you told me what that word means, but I forgot."

"Just that it was bound to happen no matter how hard you might try to prevent it."

"Are you saying I'll never be able to see you again?"

"Don't know. Maybe."

The notion he wouldn't see his friend again saddened Ethan. The broader picture that the revelation painted was one that included too many endings and not enough beginnings. His summer vacation was gone, his grandmother was sick, Rebecca had to go home, and carefree time at the creek was coming to a seasonal end, and now this.

"Don't think that way."

"There you go again; knowin' what I'm thinkin' and answerin' questions I haven't asked. It's weird. You answer questions I'm only thinkin' about and won't answer the ones I do ask."

"It's important that I address your sadness. You shouldn't feel down. Life is a wheel that never stops turning yet never plows the same ground twice."

"I don't understand that, but I'm sure you'll be telling me that I will someday."

"Yep, you will."

"How can I keep from being sad?"

"You can't look at all those events as endings; that's how. Let's just say they're course corrections. Keep your eyes on the doors opening not the ones closing. There'll be many course corrections in the years ahead, all leading to new things, different and better. But you have to believe it; it's that ol' faith thing."

"Faith, huh?"

"Yeah, faith. Now, do you remember what you need to do?"

"I think so. Let's see," he said, counting them down on his fingers, "Love, Tater, and don't be scared. Yeah, I've got it."

"One other thing; remember that doing the right thing isn't always popular. True friendship strengthens after a firestorm of disagreement. If it doesn't then you'll know the friendship wasn't true from the beginning. Are you sure you'll remember all this stuff?"

"I'll try," Ethan said, still thinking the young man might appear. He looked all around.

"You're the champ." The cottonwood bowed slightly to a cool gust then settled into a warmer but comfortable breeze.

He wouldn't be showing himself and Ethan didn't need to play hide and seek this time to realize he'd moved on.

After his mother finished the supper dishes, she went into the living room to rest.

Ethan wondered when, exactly, he'd have that promised opportunity to talk to Grandma. *I wonder if I should ask Momma to call her?* He stared at the television but only peripherally paid attention. He became antsy feeling deadline pressure to keep a promise yet didn't know how to go about it. He glanced at the clock on the wall over the television. It showed nine o'clock, bedtime for a school night. He finally gave up. "Momma, I'm going to bed."

Then the phone rang.

He waited and listened. His mother said, "Oh, hello, hon."

He recognized her pet name for his father. He watched her and saw that she listened more than talked, offering only short responses like, "I see." Or, "I understand." Not a good sign. She waved him over beside her. "Your grandma is very, very sick but she wanted to talk to you and Jessie."

Ethan took the phone as he watched Jessie come from her bedroom and stand beside their momma. He put it to his ear then hesitatingly, "Hello."

All he heard was raspy breathing then after a few seconds, "Hello, Ethan, did you have a good summer?" Her voice was weak and forced.

"It was okay I guess. I wish you could've been here."

"Me too."

"Grandma…?" He suddenly became aware of his momma's and sister's attentive eyes and ears. He cupped his hand over his mouth and whispered, "Don't be scared and don't worry. Tater is waiting for you." He glanced to his momma and wondered if she overheard. Luckily, she chose that very moment to tell Jessie something.

"I've always believed that but thanks for reminding me." Ethan was shocked that his grandma was not surprised at all by the strange comment. "Let me talk to your sister, okay?"

"Okay." He began pulling the phone away from his ear then suddenly remembered one other thing. "I love you, Grandma. I really, really do." He handed the receiver to Jessie. "She wants to talk to you." He walked away and left Jessie to visit with her. He contemplated the meaning of the message he'd delivered. He wanted to understand it; his grandma seemed to. *Who is Tater? And, where will he meet her? She's too sick to travel.* He was thankful the young stranger reminded him to tell his grandma that he loved her. A pang in his heart sent a flush of heat through him when he did but didn't know why.

Chapter Twenty

Ethan looked forward to Halloween, only two days off, a marker on the school year; the first holiday an eleven year old could sink his teeth into. He planned to do just that--into candy, caramel apples and many other sweet things. It was the gateway to the holiday season putting him on the fast track that'd crescendo to a Christmas climax.

The weather toppled longstanding records as an unusual autumn heat wave seemed to have no end in sight. To the Lee family it was a Texas-size blessing still in the making. Forced into a late second planting, Sid's expensive gamble that cost thousands of dollars had inched one step closer to fruition; this might be the rare year a killing freeze didn't come until Thanksgiving. Although Ethan wasn't prepared to uncross his fingers just yet, he did notice his father spent less time crouched in cotton rows.

"Ethan, do you realize that if a freeze came tonight, we could still harvest enough to, maybe, break even on the year? With just a little more time your suggestion may turn out to be that homerun we talked about." Every warm day passing was a few more dollars in the coffers at harvest time. Ethan heard his father joke to his mother, "Wouldn't it be the darnedest thing if, after all this praying for a late freeze, we actually had to spray defoliant to *stop* the growth cycle because a freeze doesn't come soon enough?"

Ethan laughed along with his father.

The monotony of school could only be endured, not enjoyed. Unlike Bubba Watkins, Ethan worked hard at finding something about school that might capture his interest. He became marginally interested in certain aspects of education--geography was one. Learning about different places around the world ignited his imagination, studying about it was not as dreaded as other classes. The geography teacher told the class to listen well because a test would end the week and it'd be an important grade contributor to the term score. The teacher mentioned it so frequently that he would've sworn he heard the man say it in his dreams.

In the meantime, Bubba couldn't find a thing interesting about school. He created moments to amuse himself while school went on around him; present only to fulfill his role as class clown, and darned talented that way too. It began to bother Ethan how lightly Bubba took schoolwork, spending more time entertaining the class while the teacher wasn't looking.

At the moment Bubba seemed attentive but it was a ruse to stay out of the principal's office. *Sure as shootin', he's gonna flunk that test.* Even as the final reminder was announced, Ethan watched his pal draw little pictures on his book cover, resting his cheek on a propped up palm.

The bell sounded and Thursday's class work finally ended. Bubba, true to his lackadaisical style, bolted from the classroom and raced to the school bus. Ethan no sooner dropped into the seat on the bus next to him than Bubba flicked his ear and the afternoon wrestle-fest began. Rebecca sat behind them and served as commentator and color for the goings-on between them. The three of them were rowdy and loud. At a point between headlocks and twisted arms, Ethan glanced to notice the piercing angry eyes of old Mr. Brewster, the bus driver, splitting his time watching the road then them in that big rearview mirror. Judging by the old man's angry brow, it looked as though a reprimand was coming. Ethan yanked his shirt back down over his bared belly and straightened his collar. "We'd better settle down before we get thrown off the bus."

Bubba shoved him off the seat onto his butt in the aisle. "What's the matter, scared of a little walk home?" He burst into boisterous laughter.

"Bubba Watkins!" Mr. Brewster shouted above the usual after school din of merriment, "One more stunt like that and you'll be ridin' your feet the rest of the way home."

Bubba's smile fell flat. "Yes sir."

Ethan climbed back into his seat. "Told ya so."

Rebecca snickered from the seat behind and poked her head between them. "You two seem to enjoy seeing how far Mr. Brewster's good nature will stretch."

Ethan scrunched his nose up. "Good nature? Are you kiddin' me?"

She giggled again. "I think you just discovered his limit. Congratulations."

Ethan looked back at her. She sank back into her seat, putting distance between herself and her two friends, the rabble-rousers. She nodded toward the reflection of the driver's face in the mirror. "I think he's still mad."

"Duh. Really?" He turned back and saw that the old man's angry face hadn't relaxed at all. He slid lower in his seat.

Rebecca leaned forward, careful not to attract the wrong kind of attention, and whispered in Ethan's ear. "It looks like this might be the last time you can get away with these little wrestling matches."

Ethan puffed air into his lips and snorted. "If Bubba'd learn to pay attention to what he's told and to what's goin' on around him, it'd help."

Bubba sat straight and elbowed Ethan on the arm. "Hey. I pay attention."

"Yeah, right. I bet you haven't even studied for that geography test tomorrow."

Bubba went pie-eyed. "What test?"

"Bubba!" Ethan and Rebecca said simultaneously.

"How on earth could you not know?" Ethan asked then stared disbelieving what he'd heard. "What do you mean 'what test'? The teacher's been warning us *all* week that it was coming."

"Oh." Then his shock doubled. "It's tomorrow?"

"Well, yeah, doofus."

"Oh man! Geez, what am I gonna do? I don't know that stuff."

"A little studying goes a long way."

Bubba snapped his fingers. "Hey, I've got it. Let me copy your answers during the exam tomorrow."

"No way."

"If you're really my friend, you'd let me."

"Friendship has nothing to do with it. It's not right."

The bus stopped at Bubba's house. He was forced to get up but continued staring down at Ethan with a pleading look. As he walked up the aisle, he made a point to look back with puppy dog eyes. "Why are you forcing me to look for a new best friend?"

The question was like a slap in the face. "What are you talkin' about?"

Bubba leaped off the bus.

Ethan sat stunned. An emotional metamorphosis began; from shock to anger then settling into an uneasy sense of regret. Now feeling lower than a toad, Ethan turned to Rebecca. "What do you think? Should I let Bubba cheat off me?"

"True friends help each other through bad times, like you helped me. Is there any difference in that and helping Bubba pass that test?"

"Are you serious? You think I should let him cheat off me?"

"I didn't say that. I was just wondering," she said. "Besides, I'm not going to make the decision for you. That's for you to decide. But answer this; would you save him if he were drowning?

"Yeah, but--"

"Well, Bubba's drowning in stupidity," she said then giggled.

His protest suddenly seemed pointless. His mind whirled with dos, don'ts, rights and wrongs. Everything jumbled in his head with no thought emerging as the appropriate thing to do. *Why does helping a friend seem so wrong?* Feeling cornered, Ethan looked around to see Jeremy Slater and Mikey Moore farther back in the bus. He hopped back a couple of seats to sit just ahead of them. "Guys, help me with something; if someone wanted to cheat off you during an important test, would you let 'em?"

"Good friend?" Mikey asked.

"The best."

"In that case, sure I would."

"Yeah, me too," Jeremy chimed in.

Their answers came too quick and sounded trite. It didn't help at all. He stared out the window as his head began to throb.

The brakes of the old bus squealed--the signal that it was time for him to get off. The air in the bus seemed stale and suffocating. He couldn't wait to get off and go home. As he breezed by Rebecca she said, "Hey, aren't you even gonna say goodbye?"

"See ya tomorrow," he mumbled then jumped out to the ground and the bus ambled off down the road. He tried so hard to squeeze out a solution that a sharp pain stabbed his temple. His headache had just gotten worse. He stood at the end of the long driveway to his house gazing across the neighbor's cotton field across the road trying to determine what the solution to his problem might be. He knew it was wrong to let Bubba cheat but, in this case, could allowing it be the correct answer?

He had been well trained in right and wrong but couldn't remember anything ever discussed where right didn't seem quite right and wrong didn't seem quite wrong. The in-betweens were awful. One moment he'd know what to do then moments later it'd come unraveled in his head. He didn't like the knot in his stomach or the dryness in his throat. The only one who could help would be the young man at the creek.

He trotted up the drive, dropping his backpack at the back gate to the yard and kept right on running to the creek. Arriving breathless, he took a moment to catch his breath then shouted, "Hey, where are you?" He didn't wait for an answer to begin a search. He looked behind every tree, bush and rock. "Please come out, I need held."

No answer.

"Seriously, this time I don't want to just chat. I need you." Not even a breeze rustled the leaves of the cottonwood. "Come on! You're the *only* one I can turn to."

Still breathless, the warm October afternoon streaked his face with sweat. He became frantic. The stranger had not indicated his presence at all. "I need help!"

No reply.

"I don't care what you say, just talk to me!" His lip began to quiver. "I can't do this on my own. I don't want to lose another friend. I need help. Please!" The plea echoed down the creek channel.

Ethan's fear and lack of direction funneled into anger. He clenched his fists and paced in short, quick steps along the bank of the creek. "You don't care about me!" he shouted to the treetops. "All you care about is what you want." He stopped the march and turned in a circle. "Don't do this to me!" He kept turning, around and around until he was spinning.

From up the creek a streamer of wind, out of place and out of time, shot toward him like a huge broom sweeping over the tops of the trees. But it didn't stop at the cottonwood as it had so many times before. It continued down the creek disturbing the flora on the way.

"That's not good enough!" he shouted. "I need you to tell me what to do!" He dropped onto the stump he so often used as a stool. "I know you can see and hear me. Please! Please..." His voice cracked then faded.

The calm silence of his favorite place went from comforting to eerie, tranquility gone. The feel of this place went flat and a knot moved up to his throat. He cried. No matter what he decided, it'd lose him a best friend or be ethically wrong; either way made him a loser. He desperately wanted the stranger to shoulder some of the burden. Without help from the young stranger, he was now brutally aware the decision was all his.

"I'm not even twelve years old yet. Don't make me do this alone." He sobbed. The weight of fear pushed his head over onto his layered arms upon his knees. With little hope of getting an answer, he shouted one last time, "Help me! Please!" All he heard was his own distraught voice echoing back from his favorite diving rock across the creek.

~ * ~

Waiting for the first period bell before school started Friday morning was tense. Every step he took was fraught with indecision. Even simple things didn't come automatically. *Do I take one or two pencils to class? Do I need my notebook? Have I forgotten something I should've brought from home?* Paranoia worked on him, certain he saw people staring at him. Life couldn't get any worse. He placed tremendous significance on the first bell. When it sounded, there'd be no turning back. Win, lose or draw, he must endure the entire day.

Making things worse, Bubba, Jeremy, Mikey and even Rebecca huddled together with no invitation for him to join them. An obsession was born. *I bet they're talking about me.* Every time one of them glanced, it deepened a feeling of isolation. Kids milled about but Ethan found himself alone in a bubble detached from his crew. He spent more time looking at his shoes than into faces.

The bell rang. The crowded hallway thinned reluctantly as students peeled off into classrooms. Ethan dragged his feet, not wanting to begin the day. A sense of duty kept him moving but without enthusiasm and, uncharacteristically, he was the last student to take a seat in first period English.

The class flew by. He knew the whole day would move as swiftly--until geography class, the final period of the day. That one was destined to be the longest hour of his life. Ramping dread marked the passing hours.

At lunchtime in the cafeteria, Ethan worked at making no eye contact, loaded with premature guilt. He kept to himself, although Rebecca had invited him to sit with her. "No thanks. I think I'll sit alone." It hadn't occurred to him that loneliness was of his own making.

She sat with Bubba, Jeremy and Mikey. He viewed her choice of eating companions as suspicious. It fueled obsessive fear of conspiracy, because they were the only ones who knew about the plan to cheat; or were they?

After lunch, he dropped his tray in the dirty utensil pick-up bin and Bubba bumped him with a shoulder nudge, knocking him into a sideways stutter step. "What's it gonna be?" Bubba asked. "Will we still be friends after geography class?"

Unprepared with an answer, Ethan nodded and said, "Sure...if you wanna be." When Bubba grinned mischievously, it occurred to Ethan that Bubba took that to mean he could copy his test answers."

As predicted, the day moved lickety-split until the bell rang signaling the start of geography class. The pace of the day mired into slow motion. He took his normal seat next to Bubba. Seating was assigned, so he had no choice in where he sat. He was trapped.

The teacher ordered that only pencils were to be left atop the desks, everything else placed underneath. Ethan looked to see Bubba grinning, as if all would be well. It perturbed him. *Go ahead and grin, you big ape.* As he mulled it, the face of the young stranger superimposed over Bubba's. The image of the young man repeated something he told Ethan weeks ago: "Doing the right thing isn't always popular and a friendship will only strengthen after walking through a firestorm of disagreement." He remembered something else the young man had said. "If the friendship doesn't survive then it's not real and never was."

The teacher turned his back to the class to pick up the stack of exam papers. Ethan tapped Bubba on the arm. "I can't do it," he whispered, just before the teacher turned back around.

The color drained from Bubba's face. Stiffened by shock, his pal stared straight ahead to the front of the room as the teacher placed the test in front of him.

~ * ~

"So, you decided not to let him...why?" Rebecca asked on the bus trip home.

Ethan looked to the rear of the bus and watched Bubba playing with Jeremy and Mikey like nothing had happened. He hadn't been invited to join them. "It was something that spooky guy down at the creek told me a couple of weeks ago." He kept watching Bubba.

"You trust that guy a lot, don't you? Do you really think he's a ghost?"

"Dunno. I don't think so. I do think a lot about the things he tells me though. It'd be different if he scared me. It'd be easy to believe then. But I think of him more like...well, like a member of the family. Besides, does he look like Casper to you?"

She grinned. "I guess not. Have you seen him anymore?"

"Nah, and it's not like I haven't tried. I wanted to talk to him yesterday."

A sympathetic look put a strangely mature expression on Rebecca's face. She let her head tilt as an easy smile came up.

The affectionate look captivated him. He stared into her wide caring eyes and saw genuine concern, momentarily forgetting where they were. Infatuated, he felt a tingling rush and, without thinking, kissed her on the lips.

"What are you doing?" She wiped her mouth.

Flushing from embarrassment, he stammered, "I'm sorry. It just happened. I didn't plan to do it." He quickly looked around but it took place so fast no one noticed. "Whew."

Her shock softened. "It's okay. It just surprised me, that's all. It was sweet...really."

Being called sweet didn't set well. It sounded like something his grandma would say. Grandma? His mind clicked. Gooseflesh came up on his arms. Sad thoughts flooded in, accompanied by disturbing images. He hadn't thought about her even once today but, now, he had a strange sensation that something had happened.

Chapter Twenty-one

Sid scarcely had time to take care of business on the farm after returning from the nursing home in Ardmore. Ethan hated seeing his father this way-- harried and short tempered. He did the only thing he could do, steer clear and not bother him. His mother and sister must have had the same idea. It was too quiet around the house but certainly not peaceful, relentless tension kept the air thick. Ethan took to watching his father and noticed that he seemed to know what was coming, and soon, taking care of things in double-time.

An urgent phone call from Ardmore came just after midnight Monday morning. Ethan woke hearing noise, feeling emotion swirling through the house like a wispy cloud of negative energy. He lay in bed assuming that something had happened to his grandma. He saw that the brilliant moon streaming through his window illuminated everything in his bedroom, but not enough to render color, everything in hues of blues and grays. Curiosity drew his eyes to the glowing red numerals on his bedside clock. It showed 12:38 a.m. He wanted to know more of the goings on in the next room, but instinct told him not to ask, not even move. Fearing the worst, he pulled the covers over his head as if someone might hear or see him and drew his body into a tight fetal ball, hiding away from, and steeling himself against, bad news.

The irritating electronic bleat of the alarm clock dragged Ethan from the depths of slumber, awakening to the same thoughts he'd had earlier. He didn't remember drifting off to sleep. Pulling the covers away from his face, he saw the clock now showed 6:45 a. m. It seemed like a mere eye blink since he lay in the dark worrying about the early morning phone call. Knowing he couldn't hide from the truth any longer, he rolled over and sat up then rose on sleep-weakened knees. He swayed, rubbing sleep out of his eyes and clarity into them. But his head remained muddled. Fortunately, his mother had already laid out his clothes.

Ethan was not the only one responding to his alarm clock. His momma opened his door and with no enthusiasm said, "When you get dressed, breakfast is on the table. The school bus will be here in less than half an hour. Don't dawdle, sweetie."

"I'm comin'." Ethan gleaned the unspoken message and it wasn't good. He sought courage to speak up and ask about it but couldn't.

Eating oatmeal he watched his mother engage in an unusual amount of busywork that she wouldn't normally do on a Monday morning--multiple loads of laundry, vacuuming the living room carpet and stripping sheets from beds. It seemed as if she tried to take care of a week's worth of household chores in one morning. Ethan unwittingly chose the delusional route, wondering why she did that. He lingered over the oatmeal until he heard the bus honking then took a fast swipe across his mouth with a shirtsleeve, jumped up, grabbed his backpack and yelled, "Gotta go, Momma. See ya after school."

His mother appeared in the kitchen doorway resting her head on the jamb. She smiled but without sparkle. Instead, it looked strangely dreamy. He stopped and looked at her. "What's the matter?"

"Nothing, just go on to school and have a wonderful day."

The bus honked again. He took a quick step toward the door then whirled around, dashed back and hugged her and then came the always dreaded three short blasts of the bus horn, old Mister Brewster's signal for last call before pulling away. "Go on now before Mr. Brewster leaves without you." He ran from the house without having a chance to interrogate her about that unusual look on her face. He tried putting Grandma out of his mind, diverting thoughts to school and friends.

The collective mood on the crowded bus was typically quiet. It was Monday morning, after all, and it pushed Ethan into a fast slide toward the doldrums--just what he didn't need. A happy face was hard to come by and he couldn't imagine where one might come from.

Rebecca sat across the aisle with her little brother and sister. She smiled and sighed. "Mornin', Ethan." Then she turned away, apparently no more in a mood for conversation than he, a victim too of Monday morning blahs.

Bubba got on and went to sit with Jeremy and Mikey farther back. It struck him like a tumbling load of logs when he remembered his refusal to let Bubba cheat off him Friday. *Oh lord. Bubba will probably be a real piss ant today.*

Bubba caught sight of him and his eyes narrowed to slits.

Ethan wasn't equipped for an argument and turned back to face the front. *If I can just make it through the day…*

As the day progressed, Ethan became thankful Bubba opted for no angry confrontation although his pal clearly made an effort to remain distant and chilly. For now he chose not to approach Bubba but realized he had to sooner or later. *I have to get this crap behind us.* Unable to think of any way around it, he became resigned to a coming confrontation, but not yet.

In the cafeteria at lunch, true or not, Ethan still believed himself an outcast. He sat alone. As he ate, he tabulated recent situations that complicated his life; confusing feelings for Rebecca, his head-on run-in with right and wrong in the case of Bubba's cheating, his grandma's deteriorating condition and, of course, whether to believe in ghosts or not.

Chewing a chunk of chicken fried steak, he created a well with his fork in the mashed potatoes. *Life was simpler before that guy showed up,* He huffed. But then thought, *wait a minute, he didn't make the problems, he helped me with them.* He shoved a forkful of potatoes in his mouth, and dropped his chin into his palm as he mauled the creamy spuds and swallowed.

He snapped upright in his chair. *The guy told me that the age of innocence would be in my past when making decisions became more complicated.* He rolled his eyes when it occurred to him he naively thought that kissing a girl would be the poof-factor and all would instantly change at that point, like flipping a switch, and the stranger would be gone forever. Then he remembered he had kissed Rebecca. "Humph." Ethan began connecting the dots. *It wasn't that he didn't want to show up, he really, really couldn't.* The flash of enlightenment beamed brighter yet.

Wait a darned minute. If that's true, wouldn't he have to be a ghost? He lost his appetite and pushed his tray back.

Although unnerving, the realization also created a strange euphoria. The weight on his heart lessened. But it didn't last long when he recognized another potential truth; he'd never see the young man again. *Nah, that can't be right.*

The bell rang to end lunch period rattling him back to the moment. He'd eaten practically nothing. He looked across the cafeteria and saw students crowding into a line to drop dirty trays off at the kitchen window near the exit. In that line, he saw Bubba looking at him. It wasn't a happy look either.

Waiting in the hall before geography class, Ethan stood alone, clutching his book as if it were a teddy bear. He waited for the bell, not looking forward to Friday's exam papers being handed out. *Bubba's about to get the shock of his life and it's my fault.*

Rebecca marched up to him boldly placing her hands on her hips. "Why have you been avoiding me all day, Ethan Lee?"

Spinning to face her, "I'm sorry. I've just had a lot on my mind."

"If you have problems, sometimes it's good to share them with a friend."

"Thanks. I'll remember that."

The bell rang. Ethan and Rebecca blended with the moving sea of young bodies following the line into the classroom. He continued to avoid looking at Bubba as he made his way to his desk and sat.

Then he saw a shadow cross his desk. Instinctively, he looked up.

Bubba stared, stalking him with his eyes as he plopped down in the next row.

The teacher only said, "Good afternoon class," and began delivering graded tests. He handed them out according to seat assignment. Bubba got his first.

Ethan looked over and saw the C-minus, bold and red, in the upper left corner of the exam paper. He was shocked. His buddy had passed without having to cheat. But the shock of seeing Bubba's score paled when the teacher dropped his test paper in front of him--a D-plus.

Ethan looked to see Bubba gawking across the aisle. He must not have believed what he saw because his mouth fell open and he stretched his neck for a better look. Then he laughed.

The teacher whirled around. "Mister Watkins, would you like to share with the class what you think's so funny?"

Bubba had that deer-in-the-headlight look. "No, sir. It's really not that funny."

"Then I suggest you save the laughter for after class."

"Yessir." He sat at attention until the teacher turned away then covered his mouth and let out a silent belly-bouncing laugh directed at Ethan.

Ethan had been so distracted he couldn't concentrate and nearly failed the test. Yet, by forcing Bubba to go it alone, it must've shocked him into a sharpened awareness and better score. He couldn't even pretend to be angry about it and snickered too.

A paper wad hit Ethan on the back of the head. He turned to see Rebecca with a curious expression. She mouthed, "What's so funny?"

"I'll tell you later," he mouthed right back. Ethan was suddenly cozy that his crew had survived and remained intact. Air in the classroom smelled clean and sweet; the aroma of industrial strength cleansers, chalk dust and paper was better than any old rose.

Movement from the direction of the door caught Ethan's eye. It was Principal Hadley. Entering on the tips of his toes, so as not to disturb the class, he glided over to the teacher, just then finishing handing out test papers and whispered in his ear. As he did, both sets of eyes turned towards him. "Ethan," the teacher said, "Please come up here and bring your books with you."

Ethan looked around at the questioning stares of his classmates. He gave them a general shrug. He had a notion but still pretended to have no idea what was going on.

The teacher and Principal Hadley escorted him into the hallway and old man Hadley said, "Son, your mother's waiting for you in my office. There's an emergency in your family."

Ethan walked between the two and the tap, tap, tap echo of heels in the empty hallway took on a mournful sound. They turned the corner down a side hall toward Hadley's office. Ethan's vision tunneled, seeing the office door as if through a spyglass. He already knew what the family emergency was and he didn't want to hear it spoken aloud.

Chapter Twenty-two

Sad. It was the only word Ethan knew to describe his world at the moment. His grandma had died and he couldn't yet envision a time there'd again be joy. Not only had sorrow, again, yanked him down with a thud, he felt as though a piece of his own life had been taken. The grain elevator explosion earlier in the year, and now this; there was unfairness about it all that gnawed at him. Never before had he been exposed to so many different levels of grief, so many things to test emotional boundaries and, now, he languished in despair one more time.

As he put a near perfect knot in his necktie, he noticed it had begun to fray. He'd worn the same tie nearly as often as shoes this year. He only had the one. Seeing his family in the reflection of the motel room mirror quietly dressing disheartened him. His father's stolid performance, feelings clearly kept bottled up, put on a show of strength for the family. His mother couldn't contain her feelings quite so well; tears glistened in her eyes, as they had since picking him up from the principal's office at school Monday. Shortly afterward, they had picked up Jessie and were on the highway north to Ardmore to meet his father. His mother had cried off and on since.

"How does this look, Momma?" He stood straight with his head tilted back displaying the knot-tying job.

Faye stopped her struggle with Jessie's earring long enough to look. "Fine, honey, you look just fine." She flipped a finger toward a chair. "Now sit over there and wait for us. We won't be long."

His sister even patted him on the back approvingly as he stepped by her on his way to that chair near the window out of everyone's way. Jessie's uncharacteristic show of affection indicated just how solemn this time was. He'd rather she thump him on the head and hiss snide remarks like she normally did.

He pondered never seeing his grandmother again but couldn't yet get his mind around it. Even "forever" should have to come to an end someday. Her last visit to the farm had been over a year ago, so he did feel fortunate to have had the chance to talk to her a last time on the phone.

Left with little else to think about, he became curious about the funeral. Would it be handled the same way as those after the grain elevator tragedy? *I wonder if they're any different when someone dies of old age?* He had no experience on which to base an opinion. He scooted his chair closer to the window in the cramped motel room and held one side of the faded curtains back and looked out. How odd it seemed that people walked down the street, shoppers scurrying about, cars whizzing by and life going on--all happening despite the fact that his grandma had died. *Don't they know how sad this day is?*

He wondered if when he died people would be going about their business on his funeral day as if nothing special or out of the ordinary had happened. What would the world be like when his funeral day came? Would he even know? Or does death draw down a curtain he won't be able to see through? For Ethan, death was an enigma.

"Okay," his father said. "I think we're ready. Let's roll."

The Lee family entered the small neighborhood church that his grandmother had been a member and regular attendee of. Ethan paused to look it over. After his grandpa's death, the congregation had become her extended family, whatever that meant, and went directly to the top of her weekly social calendar. Besides trips to the doctor, church had been the only time she got out of the nursing home, according to his daddy.

To call the modest gathering a "crowd" would stretch the definition. But after thinking on it, the size of the gathering made sense. His grandma was old and everyone in the church was those few friends who managed to outlive her or acquaintances from the nursing home.

The ambience saddened him. Gospel music playing low, flowers and wreaths surrounding the casket and no conversation whatsoever combined to create the mood. But it wasn't entirely the passing of his grandma that saddened him so. It was the laser-like focus on the fragility of life and how brief it is. For an eleven-year-old boy, going on twelve, it was a heavy burden to even think of, much less ponder its significance. For the first time in his short life, he thought about how fast time passes, like summer vacation; things that had never crossed his mind before. At the moment, the bend in Meandering Creek seemed as far away as the joy it represented. A yearning to be there burned in his stomach.

The service was similar to all the others he'd been to in the past few months. The preacher read scriptures, said a prayer to start and end the service, but then the preacher did something that didn't happen in all those others after the elevator explosion; he removed the flowers from the top of the casket and opened it.

What's he doin'? It took his breath away. He stared in shocked fascination at the drawn pale pink face of his grandmother that appeared just above the sides of the coffin. It could've been a mannequin from a department store. *That's her? That's my grandma? She's dead and about to be put in the ground. I'll never, ever see her again.* Until that moment, holding emotions in check had not been a problem. But that came to an abrupt end when he glimpsed her face. His own face screwed down in grief as tears rolled. He felt his father's arm come down and rest upon his shoulders. He lost control of his breathing; each breath drawn in spasms.

As family, they were escorted to the casket first. Ethan resisted. He didn't want to see his grandma up close and dead. "It'll be all right, Ethan," his father whispered into his ear. "Your grandma would've wanted you to say goodbye. I believe she's watching over us right now. You should too."

He thought about that then looked up at his father. "Really?"

His father patted the top of his shoulder and simply nodded.

His mother and Jessie stopped at the open coffin. After a few seconds huddled together, looking down into the open casket, tears suddenly came accompanied by sobs.

His father pulled gently on his arm. He reluctantly yielded to the parental tug, following his staunchly expressionless father to the casket. Ethan glanced up to his father first and saw the tightly pursed lips of a man fighting hard to ward off an emotional detonation. It spawned curious questions. Would he cry? Or did he do all his crying before they arrived in Ardmore?

At eye level, Ethan tried to look at his grandma, but it came in fits and starts. Finally, his eyes came to rest on her profile only a couple of feet from the end of his nose. Fear subsided and he became fascinated. She looked as though she were asleep--nothing more, just asleep, almost as if she'd turn and smile at him at any moment. He took the cue from his father's advice and leaned in close. "I'll miss you, Grandma."

During the ride to the cemetery Ethan began to feel better. Thankfully, the graveside service was quick. Being the only living family Emily Lee had, Sid saw no reason to linger at the cemetery following the abbreviated service. He knew none of the people except those he'd become acquainted with in the previous few days. "Come on," he told the family. "We can't do anything more here."

"Are we going home right now, Daddy?"

"Not yet. We have to stop by the nursing home and clean out grandma's room. There's hardly anything in it...a few medium sized boxes should handle it all."

The collective mood improved after they'd stopped at the motel and changed clothes then checked out. His mother spoke of things she saw along the street on the way to the nursing home--flowers, well-kept gardens and that sort of thing. His father made comments about the crop and how much he needed to get back and take care of the animals. And Jessie was...well, she was just Jessie, the drama queen that believed she had less, did less and was less than any other girl her age in the world. Things seemed to be returning to normal. Ethan drew a deep breath and watched passing scenery. Happy thoughts began to push out the bad. The swimming hole on the creek was suddenly thrust back on his mind. He missed it and longed to see the young stranger he'd come to depend on.

Sid turned onto an older, shady street. The trees on both sides formed a continuous canopy, a bright green tunnel to Ethan. Sunlight flickered in bright flashes through the branches as they drove down the street creating an effect similar to watching home movies in a dark room.

He felt the car suddenly yaw when his father steered left. Only then did he notice a street level sign that read: ARDMORE RETIREMENT COMMUNITY AND ASSISTED LIVING COMPLEX.

He unfastened his safety belt and scooted to the edge of his seat, studying the surroundings in this place where his grandma had spent the balance of her life after his grandpa had died. The last time he'd been to Ardmore was when his grandpa was alive. They had a house on the other side of town. He was five or six at the time but couldn't remember details of that visit.

Sid wheeled in and parked the car. "Okay gang, if we all pitch in, this should only take a few minutes and we'll be on our way home." No one spoke to his plan but he clearly assumed a positive response and jumped out of the car. His daddy had made arrangements to get into the room and spoke cordially to everyone he passed crossing the grounds. No one questioned his presence or the nature of his business.

Everywhere Ethan looked there were old people, many still in sleepwear. He saw wheel chairs, walkers and canes everywhere--people assisted by these appliances and professionals dressed in white aiding some of them.

Upon entering his grandma's apartment, Ethan dropped his box on the floor. There wasn't much to see. A few knickknacks on a dresser top, an assortment of pill bottles beside the bed that his father just raked off into a wastebasket and a jumble of framed pictures on top of a chest of drawers. He recognized his own family in a photo taken when he was nine and another picture of his father when he was much younger. Other pictures were clustered behind those.

His father had already begun cramming clothes into a box. It appeared he chose to do it quickly over neatly. "Ethan, since you're standing there, why don't you put all those pictures in your box? Be careful though; don't break any of the glass."

"Sure." He laid the box on a flimsy suitcase stand and set about the task. He worked slowly, wondering about each one he picked up from the top of the chest of drawers. One of his grandma and grandpa taken many years ago, he lingered over. They appeared about the same age as his mother and father now. Ethan examined every nuance of the image but it wasn't just their young appearance that enthralled him; it was the old truck, tractor and house in the background. It was the house he lived in now but it looked plainer back then. The trees he knew to shade the entire yard were barely taller than his grandfather. The resemblance of his father now and his grandfather then was amazing.

He lovingly laid it in the box atop the others and reached for another, a black and white of his grandma holding a new baby in her lap. A small boy with curious wonder in his expression stood beside the rocking chair she sat in looking down at the infant in her arms. Written across the bottom in faded cursive was a caption: Ben's first good look at his new brother.

Something about the older child he now knew as Uncle Ben looked vaguely familiar. It was his smile--something about the smile. Still looking it over as he laid it in the box his eyes went back to the top of the chest.

Ethan felt heat rise in his face and his eyes grew wide when he saw the photograph just revealed. A young man with a high and tight haircut posed formally in a military uniform with a serious, all-business look. A notation had been scribbled at an angle across the bottom: God bless you eternally, Benjamin. Beneath that in quotation marks: "My Sweet Tater".

As the young man at the creek had told him, Ethan would know in time his true identity. The reason the stranger always felt like family was because he was--Benjamin Lee, his uncle. The meaning of the message he passed to his grandma had just become abundantly clear. He repeated it, muttering, "'Tell her Tater will be waiting'." He felt the hair come up on the back of his neck as the words left his mouth. He shuddered. Ethan now fully believed. But there was still so much he didn't understand. *Why is he hanging around Meandering Creek?*

~ * ~

Late October, 20 years ago

"You're dead to me!"

"Please, Ben, don't talk like that." His mother sobbed. "You're not seeing the whole picture. Your father and I had no intention of excluding you from a rightful inheritance."

Stepping with attitude, Ben snatched his Marine jacket from the back of the sofa on his way to the front door. "I see the whole picture all right. You think more of my idiot brother than you do me. How stupid do you think I am?"

Preparing to plead her case again, a large calloused hand jerked Emily to a standstill. It was Herman, Ben's father. Supremely angered at his eldest son's lack of respect, he marched past, pushing her aside. "You hold it right there, Benjamin Alton Lee."

His resolve to leave did not waver but he hesitated at the authoritarian boom of his father's demand. Refusing to face the elder Lee, Ben held a white-knuckled grip on the doorknob, ready to bolt.

"Our decision to leave this farm to your brother has absolutely nothing to do with degrees of love and affection. It was a practical decision to keep this farm in the family for at least one more generation. Your lack of interest in farming has been more than evident. There are other ways we can level the playing field, ways that include you equally, but we haven't decided how yet, that's all." He spoke harshly to Emily over his shoulder. "We never should have spouted off about our plans until we were sure what they were."

"I'm sorry," she mumbled. "I had no idea…"

Glimpsing Sid, his younger brother, peeking from behind a bedroom door provided Ben cause to answer his father's angry tone in-kind. He gnashed his teeth so hard they squawked. "I'm a twenty-year-old Marine, getting ready to march off to God-knows-what in Granada…" Ben turned to fully face him and took calculated steps toward his unmoving father. "…and you have the nerve to tell me that you have more faith in a seventeen-year-old teenager to keep this farm in the family than me?" He spun away and started out the door but stopped abruptly wanting the final word. "You've ripped it with me. I can now leave without feeling I've left anything behind because you've proven there's nothing here for me anymore. Go ahead leave the farm to Sid. I don't care!"

His mother rushed after him.

Herman grabbed her and held her still.

She attempted to wrench her arm from his grasp.

"No, Emily. Let him go. This childish outburst just proves we made the right decision."

Emily covered her face with her hands and wailed.

Sid finally moved from the shadows to stand next to his mother and father.

Glancing back a last time, Ben glared at his little brother. "You're dead to me too." With a final sweep of an accusing finger, "I hope all of you rot!"

Hopping into his old pickup truck for the trip to the bus station, he closed the door with a fender-rattling slam and cranked it. It roared to life, amplified by the leaky muffler. Slamming it into gear, the truck spewed gravel and red dust as he over-accelerated onto the long driveway that followed the contours of the creek off to his right.

The flush of anger hadn't even left his cheeks when regret set in, occurring to him how long it'd be before he'd see them again. He looked to the peaceful cows grazing beyond that then farther down the hill to the tree-lined creek that angled to the backside of the farm. Memory snapshots paraded across his mind's-eye of happier times as a child swimming and playing in the deep pool created by a bend in that creek. *That was my special place.* He had even announced this declaration of ownership to his parents as a very young boy. He told them that that place where the creek takes a bend under a cottonwood tree--one he just knew would be huge someday, was *his* place.

The color returned to his white knuckles as he relaxed his grip on the steering wheel just as the bus station appeared ahead. A childish outburst his father had called the tantrum. Now he couldn't disagree. He thought on what he'd done and pondered ways to rectify the situation. *Dad was right; the first bad crop would be the only cause I'd need to sell it.* He slammed the steering wheel with a fist. *I'm so stupid!*

Ben turned into the bus station parking lot, creeping forward, considering returning home to apologize. The big clock on the outside of the terminal building indicated there wasn't time enough for that. The bus was scheduled to depart in less than ten minutes. He eased into a parking space, killed the engine then tossed the keys into the ashtray for his dad and Sid to find later. *I'll give them a quick call.*

As he entered the depot, the monotone lilt of the desk clerk amplified to an irritating and distorted volume issued a second call to board the bus. Hurrying to the bank of pay phones, Ben dropped his duffle bag, searching his pockets for a quarter but found nothing. Looking around for someone to borrow from, the voice echoed through the cavernous building again but this time it was a final call. "Crap!" he muttered. *I'll have to call from the base before deployment.* He considered taking a later bus but that notion was shelved once he realized his scheduled arrival time would only be a couple of hours before he'd be slapped with an AWOL charge. He had no choice but to take this bus. His mood took a dour turn. His mother had advised him to take an earlier bus. But no, he waited until it was too late to secure a ticket. He had been childish and now fully aware of that. *I have to tell them how sorry I am.*

~ * ~

"Where do you call home, Lee?" the captain asked, never looking back as he led them down a narrow rutted road in the tropical heat.

"Texas, Sir. I'm a farm boy from the cotton country of the Rolling Plains near a small town called Plainfield." Ben followed on his captain's heels. Five others followed just as close on his.

"Cotton farmer, huh?"

"Yes sir. But I'm not so sure I'll be doing that when I get out of the service." He kept a wary eye on the dense undergrowth on both sides of the road. The countryside was filled with anti-American guerillas. That intensified a sense of remorse for failing to call his parents to apologize when the hustle of preparations to ship out caused him to forget. "I have a younger brother though. He'll inherit the farm…and rightfully so, Sir."

The captain glanced back for the first time. "Are you always so humble, Private Lee?"

"No, Sir. Not at all, Sir. But, I left home in a fit of anger. I regret that. I've broken one vow to let my family know how sorry I am. I can't do that again."

"No, son you can't. Without family first, and friends second, we're nothing…no more than the equivalent of wispy fog at daybreak." Walking on quietly for a time, the captain paused and looked back at him. "No man is an island, Private Lee. Just like we're a team here, your family is your support back home. It'd serve you well to remember that."

"Yes, sir, I realize that now and--"

Boom!

"Get down!" the captain yelled as dirt rained down on them from the exploding rocket propelled grenade.

"Look!" Ben shouted, as a well-armed but ragtag militia spilled from the nearby jungle, most carrying rifles but some had grenade launchers shouldered. They streamed like ants from a disturbed mound.

Frantically searching for cover, the captain ordered, "Take cover in that shack!" He leapt to his feet. His men remained cowering on the ground. "Now, men, now! Move, move, move!"

Impulsive as ever, Ben was the first of the green recruits to jump and run. Bullets whizzed all around as he fell in behind the captain. Another grenade exploded dangerously close. The others reacted; instinct plainly telling them that running might be safer than lying on the ground.

Another explosion sent two soldiers airborne. They fell critically wounded and screaming pathetically. The rest made it to the ramshackle of a house that had apparently been abandoned in the recent past. Both the fallen men writhed in pain, but there was nothing they could do. One of the two finally went limp and silent. The other still screamed.

Positioning his remaining men at any opening available, the captain shouted, "Shoot everyone aiming an RPG at us! If even one gets off a shot, we're dead!"

Bullets hit the outside walls with the regularity of a hailstorm, many penetrating the flimsy building material.

The men returned fire, dropping those holding the grenade launchers as quickly as they could get them in their sights.

Ben felled one then swung his rifle to another but jerked the trigger, hitting that one in the elbow. His arm fell away from the cumbersome RPG resting on his opposite shoulder. He saw the attacker's mouth spring open then clench in pain.

In the span of a single second, Ben attempted to re-aim. He saw the surprised look on his attacker's face change from pain to hatred. The man forced his injured hand back to the trigger and squeezed.

The grenade launched.

Ben watched it coming at them and thought: *I just want to be home.*

Chapter Twenty-three

Ethan walked to the low picket fence around the backyard and stopped at the gate. He saw his father at the end of the cotton rows about fifty feet away, standing still, looking out across the field. "Daddy! Dinnertime!" he shouted.

Sid casually tossed up a waving hand indicating message received but otherwise didn't move. He wore his favorite lined denim jacket with the corduroy collar turned up against the Thanksgiving morning chill. He stood straight, almost as if at attention reviewing the troops; his hands rested loosely on his hips. Body language told the tale; his father was immersed in thankful silence over the family's good fortune. Although Ethan couldn't yet see his daddy's face, he already knew his smile probably couldn't get any wider.

Ethan walked over to stand at his daddy's side. "Don't mean to bug ya, but Momma wanted me to tell you the turkey's done. We'll be eating in a few minutes."

Sid drew a satisfied breath of frosty air then exhaled a white cloud as it hit the dry chill beyond his mouth. "Do you realize what the overwhelming odds are against what this cotton crop has accomplished?"

"No."

"Well...I'm not sure either. But it'd have to be about the same thing as winning the state lottery. And to get a good freeze on Thanksgiving morning...that's just icing on the cake." He laughed. "How'd you like that word choice...'icing'?"

Ethan rolled his eyes at the dumb joke but laughed anyway. He looked across the cotton field, an explosion of white covered by a sparkling dusting of frost. "Is it a good crop, better crop or great crop?" He looked up at his father. "Whaddaya think?"

"Best in years…two bales per acre, maybe more." An inquisitive look crossed his daddy's face. Earlier in the year, Ethan saw it as odd and out of place, but that same expression had been directed at him so many times this year that it'd become more normal than not.

"Your advice was good, ya know that?" his daddy said. "What other sage advice might you have, oh mighty soothsayer of pint-sized proportions?"

"What's a *toothsayer*?"

His daddy laughed. "Not tooth…sooth…a soothsayer. That's just a fancy name for a fortune teller."

"Oh." Ethan's head did the embarrassed bobble. His cold cheeks turned even rosier. Then he grinned, pushing those freshly scrubbed cheeks into a bunch, glistening in the high-contrast sharpness of the morning sun. The smile melted away as Uncle Ben crossed his mind, reminding Ethan that he'd likely never see him again. "I'm pretty sure I'll never say anything that smart again." It felt as though he'd lost two relatives at the same time; his grandma and an uncle he never had the chance to know while alive. But his uncle Ben had been more than just a relative. He was a friend, confidant and adviser and, now, the fact that he was most assuredly a ghost didn't matter. Without his presence this past summer, the disasters and near tragedies would've destroyed his family.

"That's okay." Sid patted him on the head and ruffled his hair. "It made a bad year a whole lot better. This has turned out to be a day of thanksgiving in many ways. It should make for a really nice Christmas too." He winked at Ethan.

As his father spoke of happy things, Ethan kept glancing toward the big cottonwood tree down at the creek, hoping he'd see it yield to a strangely isolated gust of wind across its top but all he saw were big round leaves abandoning their summer home beginning in its uppermost branches, drifting down, soon to leave it bare. The branchy behemoth had begun a well-deserved winter's rest.

When the summer began pieces of a puzzle neatly fit together laying the groundwork for his summer vacation. But as the season wore on, pieces were removed and the picture lost shape, leaving it distorted, but then made better when a young man sauntered into his life, changed it then vanished. A twinge of regret that he'd never see his Uncle Ben again was turning into an acidulous lump. He didn't want to feel down when everyone else in the family seemed content and happy. He heaved a frosty sigh. "Come on, Daddy. Let's go eat turkey."

Faye and Jessie had everything on the table when they walked in; his mother arranging and re-arranging dishes and silverware making the setting as perfect as she could get it. She also looked very pretty. Her usual blonde ponytail was gone and long blonde hair flowed down over her shoulders. Her makeup was perfect and she wore a dress in good Thanksgiving colors: orange, yellow and brown floral print. Even Jessie's strawberry blonde hair had sheen and she wore just enough makeup to hide the light freckles across her nose and cheeks.

"Okay," his mother said with a hand clap, "Everyone sit down and let me get a picture of this table before you ravenous monsters make a mess of it."

Snatching the camera up, she snapped pictures with the deftness of a professional from every angle all around the table. Ethan laughed along with his father and sister, poking fun at the sheer number she took. Undeterred, she continued for a time then clearly began to understand how over-the-top her picture taking must appear. "I'd better save a few for later."

Ethan was not melancholy but couldn't raise his mood to match that of the family. They laughed, joked and took good-natured jabs at one another--typical Thanksgiving dinner talk. Donning his holiday face, he joined in but it didn't come naturally. A sense of disconnection held him back--something was missing but he couldn't do a darned thing about it. Sounds of the Macy's Thanksgiving Day Parade coming from the television in the other room provided a cheery underscore to the conversation that he couldn't entirely appreciate. He had to be satisfied, taking pleasure in seeing that his family, for the moment, had no worries.

When talk waned, Ethan knew his father was about to say grace. That's when it occurred to him he wanted to do it this time. "Daddy, do you mind if I give the blessing?" Ethan watched his father glance around the table looking for support--maybe objections.

Hearing no comments, he said, "Sure."

"Go for it, twerp," Jessie whispered.

Ethan bowed his head but sat silent a few seconds wondering how to begin, and then, as if reading from a script, "God, I don't know why you do the things you do. I don't know why bad things happen. And, God, I sure don't know why some people deserve to live and some don't. But one thing I am sure of, you sent a blessing to us this year. I'm not sure what might have happened to us if you hadn't. Thank you, Father. Amen."

With head still bowed, Ethan squeezed his eyes tight and sent up a silent addendum: *and God, I sure would like to say goodbye to Uncle Ben. Could I see him one more time? Amen...again.*

"That was wonderful, Ethan," his momma said. "I had no idea you had that kind of spiritual passion."

"I might need to start calling you something besides twerp," Jessie said.

"Yeah, hotshot," his father said. "You just made this dinner better."

Afterwards, the bird was little more than a platter of bones and the family settled in for the after-Thanksgiving-dinner snoozefest and football marathon, but Ethan couldn't sit still. His mind wouldn't relax.

Pacing the hall, he tried to decide if he'd be more satisfied in his bedroom or in front of the television. Neither seemed quite right. "I think I'm gonna walk off some of this food," he announced, throwing open the screen door allowing it to slam behind him.

He scooped up a handful of small rocks, taking aim at anything making a likely target. He strolled easily, going nowhere in particular and certainly not in a rush.

The late November day was a stark kind of clear, sharply defining even distant objects. The cold front that brought the freeze left in its wake air so clear the sun penetrated right through his eyelids when he closed them. The few clouds near the horizon seemed to have been painted in the sky by hand.

Although he had no destination in mind, his feet seemed to know where to go. Finally, he stood on the banks of Meandering Creek and tossed pebbles into the water just to hear them splash. He watched with fascination at the radiating wake disturbing the near-solid covering of newly fallen leaves.

Spellbound at the sight, leaves drifted down like multi-colored snow ranging in color from green, to lime, to yellow, to brown. He sat on the ground in front of the stump he sometimes considered his throne. Falling leaves tickled his upturned face as they glided across it. The breeze carried a chill but the sun beamed warm on his face. He leaned against the stump and pulled the collar of his jacket up to warm his ears as he snuggled deep inside his coat. Sensations too magnificent for words relaxed him and he dozed.

"You've really had a change-filled year, Ethan Lee," came the voice he knew so well.

Ethan's eyes popped open. He quickly looked around and saw that the trees had all their leaves, green and lush. The air was warm, the water uncluttered and clear, like summertime. "I must be dreamin' because everything looks too darned perfect."

"Yep. If you wanted to see me one more time, it had be this way," the voice said.

The air wrinkled in front of him and Uncle Ben appeared from it. "Only one more time?"

"Afraid so. This is it."

"But what'll I do when I need help? There are so many things I don't know or understand and that scares me. I need you to stay."

"You'll never find a better problem solver than my little brother."

"Your little bro...oh, you mean Daddy?"

"Sure. But also you should rely more on your instincts. You don't realize how sharp those instincts are for an eleven year old...goin' on twelve of course." He smiled and jostled the boy's hair then dropped that arm over Ethan's shoulders.

"Like you, Ethan, I was granted a very special gift, but it too has limitations. The time I was promised has ended. Yours is just now getting underway." He cupped Ethan's cheeks in his hands and looked admiringly for a moment then winked. He turned to walk away.

"Stay with me a little while longer. Please?"

"Your prayer brought me back, but now I have to go see things *I've* never experienced. I'm a little excited about that. I might even take a little trip ahead a few years and see what planet mankind is going to land on. And then, maybe, I'll make a hard left at the milky way and go watch Ben Franklin fly that kite. Got to go, little man. I have people to see, places to go and things to do."

Ethan couldn't stop a smile from colliding with his dimples. He watched Uncle Ben walk away, hands in pockets, whistling a tune. He didn't try to follow just waved and called out, "Thanks Uncle Ben…thanks for everything."

Ben waved and kept walking and whistling.

"It'll be okay," Ethan said. The words no longer flowed from his lips but echoed in his mind. He became aware of a tickle on his face. Then he opened his eyes to see leaves sliding off his cheeks to the ground. It was the world the way it should be.

He didn't move, just looked to the sky. "Everything's gonna be okay."

Chapter Twenty-four

"Ready to go, Ethan?" Rebecca called out. "We don't want to catch that morning traffic. You know how Houston can be this time of day."

"Almost...just combing my hair." He leaned in to the bathroom mirror, fingering the lengthening light brown widow's peak, wondering if in another few years he might be totally bald. He glimpsed a young girl whizzing by the bathroom door. "Amy, get your brother and let's hit the road." Unwilling to let it go, he kept on examining his reflection. The receding hairline wasn't outdone by the crow's feet wrinkles at the corners of his eyes. He didn't think himself a vain person but sighed anyway marveling how fast the years clicked off and showed off in his face.

Walking at a harried clip until she reached the open bathroom door, Rebecca glanced in then came to an abrupt halt. "What are you grinning at?" she asked.

Startled by her sudden appearance in the doorway, he stammered, "Uh...nothing."

"Put a little snap in it, buddy. Let's load up and go."

The rose of embarrassment lit his cheeks, caught in a narcissistic moment. "I'm right behind you."

Rebecca's smile was a knowing one as she walked away. He followed her into the hall and stayed closed. Watching her walk, he admired how well she looked in those blue and green plaid shorts and sandals. *Beautiful and getting better every day*, he thought. A ten year old son and an eight year old daughter seemed to bring out the best in her, smiling some of the time, stern some of the time, mad some of the time, but happy *all* the time. She refused to ever again become as low as the summer he met her, twenty-five years ago. As Rebecca breezed by Amy she asked the youngster, "Did you put your suitcase in the car?"

"Yes, Momma."

"Good. Let's go."

Ethan looked around. "Where's your brother?"

"Waiting for us in the car."

Time had come for another June trip to grandma and grandpa's house; always a celebrated diversion from life as usual, a tradition the kids wouldn't allow him or their mother to change. Ethan couldn't imagine doing such a thing anyhow. He loved it, too--the annual escape from the monotony of life as usual. Settling in behind the wheel, "We deserve a little downtime on the farm. Right?" Ethan glanced at Rebecca then turned to look the kids in the face one at a time.

The answer was a resounding, simultaneous, "Yes," from all three.

He focused on his son in the back seat. "I don't know about you, Ben, but I think it's high time we checked to see if that ol' catfish ever came back to his rightful home on Meandering Creek." He started the engine and prepared to put it in gear.

He sighed loudly for his father's benefit. "Oh, Daddy. Do you still expect me to believe you had a pet catfish? I may be a little kid but I'm no dummy. Besides, it'd be a hundred years old by now."

"Not a pet, Ben, a friend." Ethan glanced back once more. "And, what do you mean, 'a hundred years old'?"

"It'd have to be a hundred. Wouldn't it?" he asked innocently then bounced his eyebrows and giggled. The car began to roll and the youngster turned his attention to the view out the window.

Ethan backed into the street then dropped the car into gear. They were on their way to north Texas. The kids broke out the crayons and coloring books and occupied themselves. Rebecca watched passing scenery.

Ethan saw Ben in the rearview mirror and remained in awe of how much he looked like his namesake, the youngster's great uncle. But, resemblance was not the reason for naming him after Uncle Ben; it was a decision instantly agreed to by Rebecca the day of the ultra-sound at the clinic confirming it was to be a boy. At that time, he couldn't know just how remarkable the likeness would be.

He and Rebecca had spoken little of that summer, especially about Uncle Ben. When they did it was in whispers. They both totally believed what Ethan had experienced and what she had witnessed but equally certain no one else would.

Amy pulled herself forward and poked her head between her parents. "Is aunt Jessie gonna be there, Daddy?"

"She told me she would. We'll see. Now, sit back and buckle up."

"When is she gonna get married?" Ben asked.

"She *is* married," Ethan joked, "To her career."

Jessie found a television news reporter job right out of college, moved up to an anchor position, but eventually tired of it. She later opened a small boutique advertising agency. Ethan wondered if that pregnancy scare at fourteen had been responsible, even partially, for an unending string of relationship failures.

The four-hour drive didn't seem long. As he drove into Plainfield, a profound sense of peace came over him. It happened every time they hit the city limits. Tension that had accumulated and built over time from his psychology practice melted away. By the time he turned onto the driveway of the Lee farm, he felt as though he'd been wrapped in a security blanket.

Over the years the appearance of the farm had changed little except the color of the house. "This pink stucco is so nineteen-fifties-looking," Faye had said. So, Sid had it sprayed white, and white it has remained for nearly twenty years. He did notice signs of deterioration at different places on the farm; the fence around the yard needed a coat of paint, the corrugated metal roof of the barn had rust streaks running down it and a few boards on the corral fence near the barn had broken and needed mending. There were other signs of disrepair scattered about.

Even that didn't detract from the immaculate field of cotton plants, beautifully green and orderly. Ethan was impressed but remained aware that time was against his father and the heavy day to day work of farming was becoming too much. He rolled to a stop next to the house. He put the car in park then allowed his elbows to hang loose, fingers hooking the top of the steering wheel. He sat for a moment taking it all in. After all it was home. Rebecca and the kids enthusiastically got out of the car, leaving him behind. Ethan lingered, enjoying the sight and cozy feel. He finally rolled out of the car and walked a few paces and noticed the cottonwood tree down at the creek was no longer bigger than the chinaberry trees that stood near it and displayed distinct signs of age; the foliage was no longer dense and lush as it once had been. Its days were numbered. But, to him, it would always be "That Big ol' Cottonwood".

By the time Ethan walked through the backyard gate, Faye and Sid had engaged in a round of hugs. "Ethan Lee," his mother demanded, "Get yourself up here right now and give your momma a hug."

Quickening his step, "Coming."

While Ethan still embraced his mother, Sid pulled him away, lifted him off the ground in a bear hug and laughed. "It's about time y'all decided to get back up here and see us." His hair had grown thin and wispy over the years, his belly pressed against faded bib overalls but his eyes were bright with the sparkle of good health.

Ethan flicked his chin toward the field. "It looks like you have another good cotton crop underway."

"It appears so." Sid snapped a glance back to Ethan and raised an eyebrow. "Any advice you care to share?"

Ethan grinned and nodded slowly. "As a matter of fact, I do; live well and work hard."

"Sounds good, but I was hoping for something more specific."

"I know you were."

Since the summer of '09, that solicitation of advice had become somewhat a family joke. Ethan wondered if his father secretly hoped for a glimpse into the future. Ethan saw it in his aging face and heard it in his tone. It was obvious he believed Ethan knew more about things going on that summer than mere coincidence would allow--or a finely honed intuition could offer for that matter.

Ethan still wondered when the probing questions might come about things he shared with his father back then, but it still hadn't happened. He was thankful his father likely thought it was unwise to question a blessing. Even now, well educated and articulate as he was, there would be no right words and no right way to explain it if asked. But as the years clicked off Ethan had begun to wonder if he should take a breath and tell his parents anyhow, despite what they might think or say about it. It'd be interesting, explaining a relationship and many conversations with an uncle who died twenty years before he was born. But Ethan had not arrived at a place he felt comfortable doing that and didn't know if he ever would.

Faye knelt down between Amy and Ben and pulled them close. "I have apple pie still warm in the kitchen if you want some." She smacked her lips as added enticement.

Amy's eyes grew large. "Ooh, yummy."

"Can I wait 'til supper?" little Ben asked his grandmother. "I'd rather go swimmin' at the creek right now..." He looked over at his father. "...if that's okay?"

"If your father doesn't mind, I sure don't," she said.

"I think that's an excellent idea," Ethan told the youngster. "I think I'll join you. Save my pie for later, too, Mom."

Ethan escorted his son to his old bedroom, suitcases in hand, to change clothes. It was another one of those moments as he walked through the door into that room. The curtains and the bedspread were different but everything else remained the way it was the day he left to go to college. Once he'd slipped on his swim trunks for the first time this summer, he quickly realized how snug they'd become at the waist. *Maybe I should just forget that pie altogether.* He sucked in his stomach to buckle the web belt. Finally buckled, he gave it a reassuring pat. "Okay," he said then looked to his son. "I'm ready; how about you?"

Excited, Ben said, "Yeah. Let's go."

Ethan followed the boy from the bedroom then down the hall. He hesitated as he passed the yellowing picture of his Uncle Ben hanging in an honored place near the living room door. It was the same picture he'd picked up the day of his grandmother's funeral. He let his fingers glide over the glass surface. "Hey, Uncle Ben, I know you can hear me. So...hi," he muttered. "I wish you could be here with us." He gently caressed the image with the light touch of a single fingertip then walked on.

As they marched down the hill toward the creek, Ethan found himself walking faster and it wasn't to keep up with his ten-year-old son, although little Ben did have to work at keeping up with him.

"Come on, Dad, I'll race ya," Ben said.

Ethan took one quick step and stopped but Ben was already high-tailing it toward the creek. As the boy ran, Ethan laughed and remembered: *So this is what my father saw when he pulled it on me.*

Ben slowed and came to a stop at the tree line, just then realizing his father had never joined the race. "Aw, Daddy, I thought I had ya."

"Don't wait for me," Ethan shouted. "Dive in, swim over and see if that ol' catfish is in that crack."

Ben hit the water with a splat and by the time Ethan walked to the bank of the creek, Ben was already swimming back to greet him. He bobbed to the surface. "He's there! You were right. That ol' catfish peeked out at me, wigglin' his whiskers."

"Sure he did," Ethan said, drawling suspiciously.

"I'm not kiddin'. Get in and see for yourself."

"This I have to see," Ethan muttered, diving headlong into the cool, clear water. Swimming the few feet down to the familiar widening crevice in the bottom of his favorite diving rock, he saw a catfish suddenly back deeper into the crack as he approached. *Well, I'll be darned, another catfish did take up residence here.*

By the time Ethan's head broke the surface, Ben was already asking, "Was it the same one? Was it a hundred year old catfish?"

"Sorry, buddy. It's not the same one. I don't see how it could be. But I'll bet you he'll stay in that crack feasting on caterpillars and loop worms falling out of that big ol' cottonwood all summer long."

"I'm gonna go back and see if he can get used to me so I can touch him."

Ethan climbed from the water onto the lower jutting flat rock barely above the water's surface below the diving rock. "Whew." He didn't remember playing in the creek as being this tiring. Dangling his feet in the water, he studied how the creek and everything around had changed over the years; the canopy created by the trees had totally grown together, meeting high in the middle over the creek channel. Although he could still see the house from this vantage point, the feeling was an exotic resort, not a cotton farm in Texas.

A distant voice caught his attention. He looked to see Rebecca waving and walking down the hill from the house with Jessie at her side. Sliding off the rock back into the water, he swam to the opposite bank and climbed out in time to meet them.

"Hey, Jess," he said.

Jessie smiled. "Hey, twerp."

Ethan laughed and slammed his wet body into hers and hugged.

"Hey! Get away from me. You're wet."

"Oh darn. I'm sorry," he said feigning shock then a sly grin sprouted. "Since you're already wet, how about shucking your clothes and swimming down to see the new catfish living in that rock?"

Jessie's eyes narrowed as she draped hands on her hips. "I don't think so."

Ethan glanced to see Rebecca looking to him then to Jessie then back to him. "Okay, guys, what's that all about?"

"Just a little joke I felt I owed her for calling me twerp." Ethan studied his sister. He understood why she'd been such a good news anchor and, later, an even better agency owner. She kept her strawberry blonde hair colored golden blonde and maintained a perfect figure, keen sense of humor, and a constant warm smile.

As Ethan enjoyed the chitchat, catching up on news, he noticed over his sister's shoulder and up the creek that the trees reacted to a gust of wind coming down the waterway. The sight brought back fond memories of another time--a time those wind gusts meant something--a signal.

"Hey, Daddy," Ben shouted from high on the diving rock, "Watch this." As the youngster prepared to leap from the rock, wind hit the boy. He shuddered and rubbed the chill from his shoulders then continued on with the show.

Into the water he went, sending a spray skyward that fell back with a splash. Ben immediately reversed and shot to the surface. "How was that for a cannonball?"

"I've never seen better," Ethan said.

Ben paddled on his back and sprayed a geyser of water from his mouth. "Ya know, God sure must have been feelin' good the day he created this place."

A tingle raced in a tornadic swirl down Ethan's body. His heart skipped. "What made you say that?"

Ben stopped swimming on his back and maintained buoyancy by slowly waving his arms beneath the surface. "I don't know. It just sort of popped into my head when the wind hit me up there."

Ethan turned to see the trees down the creek still reacting to the streamer of wind isolated within the channel. With a crooked grin, he thought: *This is a family reunion after all, and you are certainly a member, Uncle Ben.* He winked at the bowing trees, and then looked on thoughtfully a moment longer.

A deep sense of satisfaction settled over him. He smiled, dropped his head and turned to his wife and sister. "Y'all stay down here and enjoy the day. I'm gonna walk back up to the house; there's something I need to say to Mom and Dad..." He began, turning to walk away. "...something I should've told them a long time ago."

Also Available
By Daniel Lance Wright
From Rogue Phoenix Press

Where are you, Anne Bonny?

Captured and thrown into a steamy Jamaican prison in 1720, Anne Bonny and confederates, Calico Jack Rackham and Mary Read, are quickly convicted of piracy and sentenced to hang. A clever ruse helps Anne escape but she must leave Mary and Jack behind. On the run from the law in the Caribbean and the American colonies, Anne becomes adept at disguises... of both genders. Adventure now comes in many new forms, on land and upon the seas. But how long can she maintain such well guarded anonymity?

ABOUT THE AUTHOR

A lifelong Texan, **Daniel (Danny) Lance Wright** is a freelance fiction writer and novelist born in Lubbock, Texas now residing near Waco. He lives with Rickie, wife of 40 years and has two children and three grandchildren. Having spent the first nineteen years of his life on a cotton farm on the South Plains and the next thirty-two in the television industry, he has seen the world from two distinctly different angles. Daniel has received recognition for writing skills from The Oklahoma Writers Federation in 2005, 2006, 2010 and 2011; from Art Affair in 2008; from Frontiers in Writing in 2004 and 2010; from Writer's Digest in 2008, and the Abilene Writer's Guild in 2004; Canis Latran of Weatherford College in 2011

www.ingramcontent.com/pod-product-compliance
Lightning Source LLC
Chambersburg PA
CBHW061233170626
46809CB00007B/2650